BOUND TO THE WOLF

A GRIMM LOVE STORY

G.M. FAIRY

CONTENT WARNING

Bound to the Wolf may not be suitable for all readers.
For a full list of content warnings, please visit
gmfairyauthor.com

PLEASE NOTE

Bound to the Wolf can be enjoyed as a **stand-alone** or as a **continuation** of The Wolfish Love Stories. For a better understanding of some of the characters' back-stories, please read *The Crimson Wolf: A Red Riding Hood Love Story* and *House of Wolves: A Three Little Pigs Love Story.*

To my husband, who loves putting that dog in me.

1

EMBER

Sometimes all you need is a change of scenery. To think, just yesterday my heart raced and tears ran down my cheeks as I stuffed my duffel bags before crawling out of my two-story window into the dead of night. I silenced my quivering breath and checked over my shoulder, making my way to the old car hidden behind the shed. Of course, this escape was all planned, no matter how rushed the details came together, but the act of leaving everything behind turned out to be much more excruciating.

As I drove through the quiet streets of DC, still littered with life, I couldn't imagine what my future held. In the dark, everything feels scary and hopeless, but once dawn broke and I found myself far away from the only home I've ever known, a rising excitement bubbled in my veins.

The further I got, the more the landscape changed, from tall buildings to squatty homes to nature only sprinkled with the evidence of civilization. Of course, I was exposed to the outside world during my isolated twenty years of livelihood—television, social media, and the like—but witnessing life different than my own firsthand, even from behind a windshield, made my problems seem much smaller. Everyone had their own shit to deal with, and my escape into my new life was the least of the world's worries.

After hours of driving, sustained only by burnt coffee and discounted beefy jerky I snagged from a convenience store four hours back, the city limits come into view. "Welcome to Dayton, Washington: Population 2,248."

"About to make that 2,249," I say to myself, pumping my fist and banging it on the worn fabric roof of my car. It's cheesy, but I can't help my excitement.

I made it. I really did what I planned to do, leaving everything behind and making out into the world.

There were plenty of towns to choose from—plenty of places to fill the gaps and bring me something different, but Dayton stood out to me. Maybe it was its history. Perhaps it was an unexplainable pull after my eyes met its name during my research. Whatever the case may be, it's where I've chosen to land, to start over and prove myself to everyone who ever doubted me, which happens to be almost everyone. That's a lot to prove, and the weight of it sits heavily on my shoulders.

I shake my head, letting the nerves of everything I must accomplish wash away. I don't have a place to stay. I don't have a job, and the hundred dollars I snagged off my counter a few nights before my escape won't get me far. At least, I don't think so. I don't know shit about what things cost. It might be naive of me to run away without any concrete plans, but if I contemplated too many details, I'd never leave. Twenty years is already too long without acting for the future I want—a future where I'm capable and useful, not just a damaged and hidden ornament.

Trees meet overhead, caging me inside a living tunnel, but even in the closure, I've never felt so free. A curving road lays before me, and sunlight glints through the branches above. I tune in more acutely to my surroundings, realizing that some electronic garbage plays on my stereo. It's a song I only added to my playlist for the five-second trending audio that was all over social media. This does not fit my *majestic, starting-over* vibe. I quickly skip through the tracks, a Fleet Foxes song coming to mind that would make this scenic drive perfect. I groan when an ad interrupts my search. I don't even have enough money to pay for premium. I stare down at the clickbait text detailing something about *monsters being among us*. I glance back at the road, realizing almost too late that I'm approaching a curve.

I jerk my wheel to overcompensate for my speed and my late reaction, my insides turning to liquid. A flash of red comes into view, and I slam into a car parked on the side of the road, right after the bend. I jerk forward, my head narrowly hitting the steering wheel. Everything stills for a moment. The chaotic thrumming through my body settles, and my heartbeat thumps in my ears. I bring awareness to my body, checking for injuries, but I suspect the adrenaline is still too fierce. So far, nothing demands my attention in terms of pain. I glance around, dust settling around me and shouts coming from a distance.

I'm okay, but now that I'm not worried about myself, fear of the damage I've caused takes hold. I push myself out of my car, stumbling once my feet meet the asphalt. My mind races with horrible scenarios of the results of my negligence. To be fair to myself, I only got my license two years ago, and the only times I've been allowed to drive were when my tutor took me out to pick up extra materials for our lessons. It happened several times a month, but still, I wasn't a professional driver. I can make as many excuses as I want, but the fact of the matter is that I was distracted. This is my fault, and I have no one to blame.

I assess the car, a sob catches in the back of my throat when I realize the tiny red sports car is completely smashed, folded up like a luxury soda can. I barely notice the damage on my beat-up Volkswagen. I don't care. I run to the driver's window. No one is in the car, meaning I didn't accidentally injure someone. There's no chance of getting away with a hit and run, though, because I'm not alone. People gaze down from the top of a hill next to the road, a man runs to me, yelling profanities that echo around me. I guess I don't need to find the owner.

As he gets closer, I make out more of his features. Of course, it's a middle-aged white man. Who else would drive a car as ridiculous as this? He slows as he reaches the base of the hill, still muttering angrily but mostly to himself, I think. I still can't make him out entirely, but I can tell he's muscular and tall, hair mostly dark but with silver grays catching in the sunlight. Maybe I can offer him a blow job to get out of it. I laugh at the thought. I'm the last person to give those out. The only experience I have with the entire trade-off is through jokes in movies. My innocence might be the only tool I have at my disposal. I turn away from the man, mustering up tears that aren't that hard to produce. I'm scared shitless, and this might be the end of my new adventure, before it's even begun.

I weep into my palms, my body shaking. A large hand grabs my shoulder and twirls me around. The contact sends a buzzing through my skin, a sensation that stops completely once I meet the gaze of piercing gray eyes.

2

GRIMM

Red. All I see, all I feel, all I smell is red. This week—or month, or year—is just one shit-storm after the next. Seconds ago, I yanked at my hair, kicking myself for not protecting my pack better. Even though a major crisis has just been resolved and the Weres seem to be safe for another day, I'd almost ruined everything through my negligence and misguided instincts. I'm off my game, probably due to my role as Minister with little to no help. Not that everyone doesn't attempt to offer me a hand. I'm just too stubborn.

Finally, everything seemed to be working itself out. A crisis was averted, and Were-women were saved, but then the burning of rubber and smashing of metal brought my attention to the base of the hill, where just moments ago my brand-new car had been parked. Now it's just a piece of smashed, smoking metal attached to a brown shit stain of a vehicle.

All this time of stress, and I've had no one to take out my frustrations on. Of course, I wish I could smash the skulls of some Hunters, but I'm left behind the scenes, doing the paperwork, being the level-headed leader everyone needs. Now there's someone I can yell at, someone to blame for my new and overpowering rage.

"What the fuck is wrong with you?" I grab the shoulder of the woman who caused so much damage, twirling her to me. Her bright green eyes, wide and red-rimmed, stare into my soul. What was I thinking? She's just a girl, in her early twenties from the looks of it, and I just put my hands on her. An apology rests on my tongue, but I'm frozen. I sense a shift on the edge of my control. It's odd. I've had my powers managed since I was in my mid-twenties—two decades ago. Perhaps the stress really is getting to me, making me weak and unable to control myself.

It's more than that, though. The girl is beautiful, long white-blonde hair a cage around her small frame, her pale skin without flaw. She's shocking to look at, almost otherworldly, but that shouldn't matter to me, regardless of the warmth in my chest. God, what the fuck is wrong with me?

Thankfully, she saves me from my warring thoughts, her face subtly scrunching into a look of repulsion. It makes sense. I did just run down to her, cursing the whole way, and swing her to me like she was a petulant child instead of an adult stranger, but her expression reads more than that, even if it was only there for a flash. Perhaps it's my age that alarms her. I'm not ancient, and others say I look pretty good for early-forties, but still, I'm old to her. Or it could be that I'm shifting more than I realize. Why the fuck do I care what she thinks about me?

I take a step back, regaining my control and clearing my throat. She unfreezes from her stupor; the previous tears I pulled from her returning. "I'm sorry. I didn't mean to. I just looked at my phone for a second and didn't realize the bend was coming up."

Why would she admit she was looking at her phone? It infuriates me further. She could have hurt someone. Yes, she may be young and naive, but it's not an excuse to risk hurting someone—or hurting my brand-new Porsche that had grown to be the only shining beacon in the clusterfuck that is my life.

I shove my hands in my pockets, attempting to keep my rage at bay. "Well, it's pretty clear that this is your fault, so let me just have your insurance information. We don't need to get the police involved." It would be easy to elicit the help from the authorities. Many of them are right over the hill, but they're dealing with greater issues—clearing out a Hunter science torture chamber and attempting to collect evidence on the group that has caused my people so much pain. Most of them aren't local police, though. Only a few are privy to the information about the Hunters and werewolves. Regardless, none of the officials in town have time for these small peanuts, even if it involves my cherry red, beautiful work of engineering.

"Information?" she poses as a question.

My attention flicks to her. "Car insurance, licenses." I snap my fingers and extend my hands. I'm an asshole, I know, but I can't help it. All my reserve is focused on not turning into my wolf form and gobbling her whole.

She shakes her head, eyes leaking. "I don't have those."

"What? How old are you?"

"Twenty." Thank God. Not that it makes it better that I must shove down the twitch in my pants—the desire to bend her over my knee and teach her a lesson surfacing in the corner of my mind, but it's *much* better than if she were younger.

"Why are you driving without insurance or a license?" I can't hide the growl at the back of my throat. To my credit, I keep my distance. Even if I can't keep myself in check, she doesn't deserve to feel scared for her life.

"I...I..." She can't finish, just turns into a blubbering mess, still strikingly beautiful, but pathetic.

"What's going on here?" Cameron jogs up beside me, grabbing my shoulder and looking between the two of us with a mischievous smile. I'm thankful yet annoyed he's butting in, part of me disappointed my primal rage can't come out to play, and the rational side of me relieved another pack member is here to keep me in check.

I throw my hands in the air and slap the side of my thighs. "No insurance. No license."

"Yikes," the dark-haired male says with a chuckle, folding his arms over his chest. What's so funny about this? He's not helping—if anything, he's driving me crazier.

I turn my attention back to the quivering mess of a girl. "Do you have money to pay for this?" I point to my car. I already know the answer, but it's the next obvious question.

"No." She whimpers. "I only have a hundred dollars. I don't even have a place to stay. I planned to live in my car until I found a job and made enough for a motel in town."

I can't help but notice her clothing—a simple, white, linen set. I appreciate the finer things in life, and I know that her apparent brandless outfit is worth much more than the only hundred she claims to have. I want to point this out. Sure, her car is a piece of crap, but there has to be someone she can call to make this right. But I move on. It's not my place to pry, and I don't have the time or willpower to pull the solution out of her.

I sigh. "Alright then, I think we need to get the police involved." I turn to walk back up the hill and see if Brick can call someone from the station, since he's the sergeant of the police force.

"Wait, no. Please!" She steps closer, her hands clasped and her eyes desperate. "No police. I'll do anything."

Clearly, this girl is troubled—young, oblivious to the world around her, without support, and a foxlike beauty to her that only calls to mischief. Perhaps she's running from something, but what am I to do about it?

As if reading my mind, Cameron steps in between us. "I've got an idea."

I groan. He's a good man, having helped protect our pack for most of his life as the Human Liaison, and now he has a wife at home due any day. He doesn't have time to toy with me, but somehow I sense a game playing behind his dark eyes.

"Let's hear it." I prop my hands on my hips, glancing at the hilltop to notice Agent Brown, the representative flown in from the Department of Supernatural, talking to another officer and looking down at us. It's clear I'm needed. And yet, here I am. Dealing with this shit.

Cameron goes on. "Well, you have an empty guest house and are looking for a new secretary since your nephew left for college. Why don't you have the young lady... I'm sorry, what's your name?"

"Ember," she replies quickly.

"Ember, nice to meet you. Yes, why don't you have Ember move in and work for you until she can pay off the damage?"

I scoff. "That's fucking stupid." I've wasted enough time with this. Police it is. I turn to walk away, but Cameron grabs my arm. "I can't see why not. You've been complaining about needing a secretary. The police aren't going to help you. You heard her, she doesn't have any money."

"Grimm!" My name travels from the distance, Agent Brown motioning me over.

I pull at my hair and groan. "I don't have time for this!"

"Exactly. You don't have time for anything. That's why my plan is perfect."

I glance between Cameron's mischievous mug and Ember, who looks like a deer in headlights. It's so stupid. I'm not even sure it's legal to force someone to work to pay off their debts. Not to mention the biggest red flag—having a human stranger live on my property and deal with the paperwork related to my pack. I'd be asking to expose everyone's identity, to make us bigger targets for the Hunters. But why am I entertaining the idea? Why am I not shutting it down and running off to my real responsibilities? Instead, I'm working out the details, warring with reason for how this could work. My guest house is on the other side of the lake on my property. She wouldn't be able to see into my house from the lodging. I could always give her trivial responsibilities—ones I never have time for but that would take a boulder off my shoulders—without revealing too much. Besides, she doesn't seem like a sleuth. I could devise enough misdirection to keep her in the dark.

There are a million holes in this plan, and I can't even needle through at the moment. I can feel Agent Brown's impatient glare on the back of my head, not to mention all the tasks I must do now that we've rescued the missing Were-women and defeated another one of the Hunters' schemes. It's never over with them, and I must prepare for the next attack.

"Fine." The words are foreign from my lips, but I've made my decision. I pull out my phone, looking for the local mechanic's number. "I assume your car isn't drivable." It's way better off than mine, but the front is smashed in, and from my little experience in mechanics, I make an assumption. "I'll call a tow truck for both of our cars. Cameron, take her up to the house and show her around."

"Wait. No!" Ember's voice surprises me, and I trail my eyes away from my screen and up to her more formidable posture. "I'm not going to live with you and work as your servant. That's crazy!"

She's right, and it gives me some comfort that she's not a total beautiful, walking airhead. "Got any better ideas?" I ask.

The wheels inside her mind crank, her shifting eyes the motors, but she doesn't respond. I could wait longer for a better suggestion, but I don't have time. I press the contact and put my phone up to my ear. "The way I see it, I just solved your problems. Now you have a place to stay and a job. You can thank me later." I wink and walk away from the scene.

"Wait!" she yells from behind me. Cameron's voice interjects, and I don't need to turn to know he's handling the situation. It's the least he can do after suggesting the asinine idea. My brain pounds in my skull as I add more tasks to my never-ending to-do list, the new points all involving a ghostly girl ramming into my life like the car crash she caused.

3

EMBER

What the fuck am I doing? I keep asking myself the question over and over again, and yet I continue to move forward—placing my only belongings into the truck of the dark-haired man I just met, and letting him drive me to an unknown destination. To his credit, he seems nice, smiling and cracking jokes as he senses I'm mere seconds away from a mental breakdown. As he turns down a dirt road, yapping about his wife and all the intricacies of her pregnancy, my hands clutch the door handle, fighting the urge to fling myself out and run back to where I came from. It would leave me with nothing, but at least I wouldn't be traveling further within the woods to live with a man who looked like he wanted to chop me up into tiny pieces and toss me into a stew.

We continue to delve deeper; civilization is nothing but a concept with each turn of the tires. My mind plays catch-up with the avalanche of events. I haven't been given a second to think my decision through until now. How will I know when my forced servitude is up? His car probably cost around $60,000. It will take me at least a year to work that off, and that's if he thinks I'm worth that much and gives me no other compensation. Who am I kidding, though? This isn't a normal business transaction. I just tangled myself into a world of trouble, and I must find a way out. How can I escape once I make it to wherever he's taking me? I won't even have a string of an idea until I see the place. I imagine being locked in chains, thrown into a dark and damp cave, fed scraps, and performing whatever sick tasks he has for me.

I wish I had come to these terrifying conclusions before I trapped myself in the car with this unknown man, but of course, I had no other options. I either go with this Cameron character, or I get carried off by the police and sent back home. Maybe that would be better, though. At least my last prison was familiar. It's too late now, though, because as we turn a corner, a massive clearing surrounded by large trees with a expansive A-frame wooden house situated at the far end of the property comes into view. "Here we are!" Cameron says, driving up the paved road that curves around a crystal blue lake at the center of the property.

"Holy shit," I say, pressing myself against the window. I should have figured that a guy who drove such an expensive car would have an equally luxurious house, but the lodging, so secluded and grand, only puts me more on edge. "What does this guy do for a living?"

Cameron doesn't answer at first, clearing his throat. "He'll have to explain it to you. It will likely be part of your orientation."

I glare at him, arms over my chest. "So he's into illegal shit?"

Cameron laughs. "No, nothing like that. Grimm's a good guy."

I scoff.

"Okay, you caught him in a bad mood. You did wreck his brand-new car, and might I remind you that he offered you a house and a job after doing so?"

My cheeks heat. I'm ashamed that I caused such damage. I genuinely feel bad for my mistake, but I'm not at all grateful for my deal. No one does anything that doesn't benefit themself. Grimm didn't offer me this compromise out of the kindness of his heart. I'm just too vulnerable to do anything but accept it.

"Don't worry. You'll likely find that Grimm will become something like a father to you. He is to the rest of us."

I want to ask about the rest of *us*, but I'm too distracted by his description of the terrifying man as a *father*. I don't know Grimm's age, but from the salt and pepper hair and the fine lines at the corner of his eyes, he could very well be old enough to hold that position over someone my age. But normal dads look nothing like him. Even if I already hate the guy, I can't deny he is hot, as much as it sickens me to think so. He's nothing like my own father in many ways, but in some ways, I sense similarities.

Cameron pulls up to a small cottage at the other end of the lake facing the main house. "Here we are!"

he says, parking his truck and running to the back to pull out my two bags. I exit the vehicle on shaking legs, letting the cool breeze and the sound of untouched nature settle me for a moment, closing my eyes and breathing deeply.

"So, you're running away from something?" Cameron's voice knocks me out of my trance, rattling me further as I pop open my eyes to find him standing inches away from me with my bags in hand.

"Jesus Christ!" I press my hand on my heart.

"Hey, calm down. You're safe here. I know it's an odd situation, but you're lucky you ran into that Porsche. Any other fucker and you'd be SOL. You look like you need an ounce of safety."

I grab my bags from him. "You don't know me. I'm not running from anything. I just wanted a fresh start."

He rolls his eyes. "Alright. Well, let me show you around." He turns to the cabin, climbing the steps and opening the wooden door. "Grimm keeps this place stocked just in case anyone needs somewhere to stay." He opens cabinets full of cooking equipment and canned food to confirm his words. "I've stayed here a night or two before I met my wife, if we were working late. It's a pretty comfortable bed, and nothing beats the lake view in the morning."

"You work with him?"

"Oh yeah. He's my boss too."

I drop my bags to the floor, crossing my arms over my chest. "So you should be able to explain to me what operation I'll be working for then?"

He laughs. "You're funny. Here, let me open the windows for you. The breeze at the end of the day is magnificent." He opens wooden shutters above the sink of the charming kitchen area, and a gust of wind flows through the space, catching me off guard and bringing my attention to the space around me. I'd been so busy trying to get more answers from Cameron about why I'm here that I hadn't noticed the simple yet beautiful cottage that I'll be calling home for God knows how long.

Quilts drape over a comfortable beige couch. Cameron opens another window parallel to the seating area, letting in a fresh breeze and revealing a picturesque view of still waters, the setting sun melting atop the glassy surface. I could stare at the view all day, but I travel away from the common space and venture into the bedroom visible from across the small room.

It's simple—a full-sized bed with a matching quilt comforter from the one on the couch. Two wooden side tables sit on either side of the bed, and an antique-looking dresser rests at the front of the room. Of course, there's another large window with yet another incredible view of the lake. There's a small bathroom connected to the room, with tiny white bottles of soaps and lotions on the wooden countertop.

I step back out into the room as Cameron enters, placing my two bags at the end of the bed. "Well, what do you think?" he asks, with a knowing smile on his face.

"It's not the sex dungeon I had in mind, so better than I expected."

He gives a surprised laugh. "I told you. Grimm's a good guy. You don't need to worry about him taking advantage of you." I can tell he truly believes that. I just know it's not the real truth. He's a man. I'm a young woman without any resources. Maybe Grimm makes him feel safe, but it's not the same for me.

I nod. Nothing else to say.

"Well, I'll let you get settled. Here, let me give you my wife's number, so you can have another woman to talk to if you need anything."

"No thanks." He means well, offering a female contact to put me more at ease, but I don't need to converse with another person in their weird group. Whatever they've got going on, I want to keep my distance as much as I can.

"Alright!" He throws his hands up in surrender and exits the room. "See you at work." And with that, I'm alone in my new prison. It may seem like a dream getaway, but I know the truth. Behind these quilts and Tempur-Pedic mattress hides a man ready to prey on my weaknesses. Perhaps it beats sleeping in my car on the side of the road and working as a gas station custodian or something, but I know the truth. I'm sleeping right next to a monster.

4

GRIMM

Angelo, one of the most trusted members of my pack, drives me home. He insists on it. I struggled to contain my true nature for the rest of the evening and well into the night. It would have been impossible to drive. I can barely contain myself in my human form. He must have noticed my struggle, and I'm thankful to have such a helpful pack member.

I glance at the clock above my stove as I toss my keys onto the marble countertop. It's two in the morning. I groan. I have a council meeting at 8:00 a.m. tomorrow. I'm an idiot for setting it that early, but it's too late to reschedule. Besides, it's needed. This isn't the first time we've defeated a group of Hunters. The conflict goes back centuries. The Hunters were once a well-known group, revered for their ability to hunt and defeat "monsters," but my people persevered. Of course, now we must keep our identities hidden. It's my job as Minister of the werewolf pack here in Dayton to keep my people safe.

Cameron works as the Human Liaison, a title given to the most powerful, whose identity is never hidden from special law enforcement and ultimately, always leaks to the Hunters. We almost lost him not too long ago, but he and his wife, Red, defeated the Hunters and killed their leader. Well, at least the leader of the Dayton Hunters at the time. A new head always rises from their stubby neck, and it wasn't long before Kilo, a part-werewolf scientist sent here to experiment with stealing the powers of werewolf women, showed up and wreaked havoc while taking lives.

It was my fault that Kilo infiltrated my group. I trusted him too readily and didn't see the signs of his danger. Thankfully, Cameron's sister, Carmen, and her newfound mate, Sergeant Brick, helped defeat the group and rescue the women hidden in their science facility. Even though Kilo is dead and his plans foiled, it's not over yet. It's never over. Most of the Hunters got away, and of course, none of them are the true leader of the terrorist organization. It's likely someone high up in power who's able to cover up the crimes of the local and federal government in the name of the Hunters' cause. Tomorrow will not be a day of rest or rejoicing, regardless of saving the women. I must prepare for their next attack. I must be ready this time.

My stomach growls, and I weigh my hunger against my exhaustion. I pull open my fridge, scanning for an easy meal. A light catches my attention at the other end of the lake.

I shift, not completely, still standing upright on two legs, but claws burst through my fingertips, and my muzzle forms around my growl. I'm seconds away from leaping out the kitchen door and attacking the intruder of my guest house. My senses are heightened in this form, and my eyesight shifts through the darkness, making out the petite figure curled in the rocking chair on the front porch.

Shit. Ember.

I'd almost forgotten the car crash and the young woman now thrown into my line of responsibilities.

I shift back to my human form, running a heavy hand down my scratchy face. I shut the fridge. My hunger has left me, and now I'm consumed by my new responsibilities. "What the fuck did I get myself into?" I ask the lonely darkness of my expansive kitchen. Perhaps Cameron was giving me more time to figure out what to do about my car, or, more likely, he was just trying to needle himself into a situation he thought would be good for me. Regardless, I agreed to the compromise for some reason. I watch her silhouette from a distance, concluding that she fell asleep on the front porch.

I think about how she must be feeling. I must seem like a psychopath. I was raging, cursing, and grabbing her by the shoulder. A normal man would have let the police handle it or insisted she call someone who could help her out. I essentially forced her to live in my guest house and work for me, at a job she knew nothing about. She's probably too frightened to sleep in the bed—sure I'm watching her like a creep.

I pull my phone out of my pocket, scanning my messages for the first time all day. Sure enough, I have a text from the mechanic. My car is totaled, unfixable. Ember's car may look better, but it was on its last leg before the accident, and now it's toast. Great. I sigh, throwing my phone on the counter as I sit on a stool parallel to the window so I can still watch Ember's form from the window.

If I were a better man, I'd go to her in the morning and figure out where she came from, arrange for a way back home, and worry about the details of my car later. Besides, I have my old Ford pickup in the garage. I have transportation. I'm just now, without my desperate plea to feel young again—my mid-life crisis materialized. Unfortunately, I'm not a better man. I do need a secretary. I'm not hurting for money, but I will be if I must hire someone and purchase a new car, because goddammit, do I need my luxuries right now. Perhaps there's another reason I want to keep her around, one I won't address and I'll just attribute to my animalistic side.

I pull my phone closer, deciding I'll go through the new messages from today before heading to bed.

Have you seen this? It's a message from Carmen. She works for Red at the Dayton Daily, so she's always the first to know an inside scoop, but I'm surprised she had the time to send me this. After I ran down the hill to my demolished car, she and Brick ran off into the woods. I figured she wouldn't have a second to breathe, let alone send me videos, since they're in the midst of their mating frenzy. But she's devoted to our pack as much as I, as much as any of us, so it's not too surprising.

I click on the link. It's a shaky home video from the perspective of someone hiding behind a tree line; their camera focuses on a teenage boy in the woods. The boy looks around before shifting into his werewolf form and running off into the distance. The camera cuts off. It's not the first video I've seen of a werewolf transforming, and it won't be the last. The unnerving part of this one is that it is real. I could tell that it wasn't just editing magic. The woods look familiar. I doubt it was taken in Dayton, but it could be close. I click on the profile of the uploader, finding no profile picture or bio, just a username with a string of numbers and letters. I thumb through the comments. Some people, presumably gullible older individuals—people around my age—comment on the video's authenticity, but the majority of the views seem to agree that it's a fake, or AI-generated. My chest deflates a little.

Seems like no one believes it. I shoot a text back to Carmen, hoping she doesn't read it until well into the morning.

It's good she sent this to me. We need to discuss being more careful when we shift at the meeting tomorrow. The young are often the most vulnerable, reckless, and unable to control themselves. It's the older generation's job to guide them and show them the way.

I click off my phone and head into my bedroom, my mind scrambling with the different faces of my pack, my people that need protection. A new face emerges—piercing green eyes and white-blonde hair. For some reason, I can't erase her image as I fall into slumber.

5

EMBER

I awoke early in the morning, having fallen asleep on the rocking chair. Cameron was right. The breeze over the lake is fucking fantastic, and once my body settled from the adrenaline rush pumping through my veins from the hectic string of events, I passed out. My neck ached from the unusual sleeping posture, and a few more hours of tiredness needed to be shaken off my bones. I stumbled back inside the cottage, falling into the bed and curling up around the quilt. Damn, the mattress was comfortable.

When I wake again, my phone on the bedside table tells me I slept most of the morning away. It's nearly eleven. I can't remember the last time I woke up so late. I shuffle across the shiny hardwood floors on socked feet and rummage around through the kitchen cabinets, quickly finding the coffee pods and the instant coffee machine on the kitchen counter. Once it's finished brewing, I bring my steamy cup back out onto the porch, taking a sip as I settle back into the surprisingly comfortable rocking chair.

I'm so well rested that for a moment, I pretend I really am on a much-needed vacation. Something stirs in the distance. I sense an animal, but I can't make out what kind entirely, so I stretch my ears. It's only a bunny, scampering across the grass about a hundred feet away.

Reality sucker-punches my conscience as I catch Grimm heading toward me, trailing the edge of the water. He's not close, only a miniature growing larger as he erases the distance, but I can already feel his anger. I straighten, shoving down my senses, feeling my head to make sure I'm back in place. He moves quickly, but my heart beats wildly for what feels like a lifetime.

I pretend to be at ease as he approaches, sipping my coffee and staring out across the lake. He walks up the steps and clears his throat when I don't look at him. I remain stoic, which infuriates him further. I refuse to catch his gaze, but his frustration is palatable.

"Did you just get up?" he asks.

"Yes."

I catch him out of the corner of my eye, glancing at his watch. "It's nearly the middle of the day."

"So."

"So? You're supposed to be working."

I turn my attention to him now. "I was never given a schedule. How was I supposed to know that?"

He nods, his features softening, and he runs his hand through his hair. Bags cage his eyes, worse than they were the day before. His hair is neat, slicked back, but his face remains unshaven—stubble just poking from the surface. I'd think it was just a grooming choice, but I can tell he's usually clean-shaven. Unfortunately, he's still handsome—the ancient bastard.

"Right. Sorry," he says, his eyes shifting away from mine. "I've already been running around all morning. We need to go into the office and get started. My to-do list is piling up."

"Do you know anything about my car?" I'm hoping he means I'm following him in my vehicle. I don't want to be forced into a cramped space with this man. This porch is already small enough.

He squints an eye at me, grimacing. "Yeah, it's dead. So is mine." He doesn't have to say it. I can read him. He can't believe I'd be so selfish in asking about my shitty car before inquiring about his. Perhaps if he didn't somehow coerce me into being his slave, I'd feel guilty about my selfishness, but I don't give a fuck how he views me. Maybe if I annoy him enough, he'll let me go.

My stomach rolls. I'm trapped—without transportation. "So how will we get to the office?"

"We'll walk." He turns toward the steps, motioning for me. "Are you ready?"

I trail my eyes over my gray sweatpants and navy DC sweatshirt, looking back to meet him as my answer. He groans. "Well, come on. Hurry up and get dressed."

"I'm not hurrying," I grumble, rising and slapping my feet against the ground as I enter the cottage and slam the door behind me. Cameron was right. I *am* starting to view Grimm as a father, but one belonging to an unrealistic teenage movie character. I'd never had this kind of interaction with my own father, but it feels both nostalgic and annoying at the same time.

Despite my words, I do dress and get myself ready for the day as quickly as possible, hiding in the darkest depths of the shallow closet since I'm still not entirely sure he hasn't bugged the place.

When I emerge from the cottage not even ten minutes later, Grimm stands ramrod straight, tapping his pointer on his forearm and jumping into step the second he sees me. "Alright, let's go." As if I took an hour instead of mere moments.

I have an enormous list of questions for him, each one more pressing than the next, but he walks as if he's trying to create as much distance as possible. "Wait!" I yell, stumbling to catch up, but if anything, he quickens his speed. I grunt, turning on the part of myself that accelerates my steps. He startles when I appear next to him. "Where are you going?" I ask, anger lacing my words.

He finally slows, and I'm able to walk at a more casual speed. "Should I continue to expect you to ask questions you already have the answer to? I said the office."

"Cameron seems to think you're a good guy. You've been nothing but cruel to me."

"Cameron's never totaled my car before. Besides that, all you've been is unapologetic and ungrateful."

I scoff. "Ungrateful? Why would I be thankful that you basically forced me to work as your servant?"

He continues walking, not meeting my eyes as he continues to barrel through the woods. "You're not my servant. You're my employee."

"Sure, employee for a job I'm unaware of. What kind of office is in the middle of the woods anyway?" At my words, I absorb my surroundings. I hadn't been paying attention to where we were heading—a horrible idea when following an intimidating and huge man into the forest.

Grimm must notice me losing my previous venom, because he slows his steps and softens the edges of his words. He turns, looking me in the eye. "It's nothing nefarious. I'm the president of Dayton's Wildlife Preservation Organization." He motions to a large stone formation. "This is the office. It's camouflaged and hidden in the woods so we're able to keep track of poachers."

I study him. Not a hint of a lie on any of his features. I scoff. "You must really think I'm stupid then. You have enough money to buy your house and your fancy sports car because you helped save a few deer in one of the smallest cities in the country?"

The fire returns to his eyes. His face isn't as wrinkled as I imagine someone his age should be, but I'm sure after a few more weeks of dealing with me, that will be fixed—the lines between his eyes deepen. "Believe whatever the fuck you want, but this is where you'll be working. Let's go." He hurries forward, knocking on the stone wall in a rhythm. When a section pops out, revealing a door, I wish I had paid closer attention to the pattern.

He ushers me into the dark cavern. I hesitate, because who would be stupid enough to eagerly walk into a hidden stone building in the middle of the woods? He sighs when I don't move. "Fine. Stay out here, but wolves are active in this region, and the poachers have been stealing all their food. You might find yourself next on the menu."

I'm a scaredy cat and follow after him. I'd rather the monster I'm familiar with than the one unknown. It takes a moment for my eyes to adjust to the darkness of the hallway, but once I do, I'm even more skeptical about entering. "Gee, it sure looks like a regular office in here," I say, eyeing the torches adhered to the stone walls and registering the dripping water sounds in the distance.

He shrugs. "We like to keep a theme. If we're going to look like a secret ancient dungeon from the outside, why not do the same on the inside?" He walks onward, passing several ornate, curved wooden doors. There's no one else in our path, but I hear murmurs and laughter behind closed doors and somewhere off in the distance. It settles me slightly. At least other people work at this facility.

When he reaches a door near the end of the long hallway, he opens it and ducks inside. "This is my office." He gestures to the space, which comes to life with lights as we enter the room. Surprisingly, it looks like a normal office, neither super modern nor a medieval torture chamber as the hallway suggests. There are shelves filled with books, filing cabinets, a wooden desk with a laptop, and even a large window that offers a view of a bustling city skyline. I point to it. "Why?" Obviously, it's a screen or some sort of projector.

He shakes his head, clearly annoyed by my one-worded question. "Perhaps, I like to give my office the illusion that it has a view."

"Maybe just get a normal building with windows then."

He groans, shoving past me and leading me to the room right next to his. "This will be your office." His voice is void of any joy.

"I get my own office?" I step into the room, turning to see it from all angles. It's simpler than his. There's no artificial skyline, and the desk is less bulky, but there are hardwood floors, a floor lamp already on in the corner, and an empty bookshelf.

"Yeah."

"Surprising."

"Why?"

"I thought I'd be working in the torture chamber."

"Funny. That's on the other side of the building, though." He doesn't laugh. "Alright, get to work."

"Wait!" I yell before his fingers leave the doorframe. "What am I supposed to do?" There's still so much to ask, mainly how long this deal will last and whether I'll be allowed any days off. How will I get around? Will I be paid an additional salary? But the man can barely stand being in the room for more than five seconds with me. I must gather the most important information first.

He groans, most of him still hidden by the wall. "One sec." His footsteps lead to his office. Two minutes later, he's back with a shoebox. "Organize these write-off receipts." He plops the box on my desk and turns to stomp out.

"Organize them how?"

He spins toward me, eyes vast and wild. "I don't fucking care. Organize them alphabetically, by date, whatever!" He's different. The same terrifying man as always, but his once slightly unshaven face is now fuller. His eyes almost glow, and the buttons on his shirt seem like they're about to pop off him. I freeze, watching as he registers his change and unfit reaction to my question. He turns quickly and races out the door without another word.

I'm left alone in my strange office, working for a man who I'm more sure is a monster now than I was before.

6

GRIMM

It's been two weeks since the car crash. Two weeks since Ember has been staying in my guest house and working as my secretary. It's been a fucking nightmare. Cameron was an idiot to suggest this idea. I've had to rearrange the entire organization to keep Ember in the dark, further adding to my never-ending to-do list, which is not getting shorter since I can barely give Ember tasks without risking blowing our cover. I should fire her, cut my losses. Turns out I missed driving my 1970s Ford pickup. The sports car wasn't me, no matter how hard I tried.

Most days, I catch her, feet propped up on her desk, scrolling on her phone. It enrages me, and I yearn to teach her a lesson—something besides letting her go. Except, of course, I should let her go. That's the reasonable thing to do. She'd be thrilled to know she's off the hook, even if I am providing her with a comfortable place to stay and a weekly paycheck on top of allowing her to pay off her debts. She hates me. It's obvious. Every time I'm near, I can sense the venom boiling in her veins. It does something to me I can't name. Of course, I haven't been kind to her, at least not with my words or when I'm in her presence, but just seeing the hatred dripping from her pores teeters me over the edge. I've never been the type of man to allow my pride to take over my reason. It would make me a piss-poor leader if that were the case, but with her I'm someone entirely different—someone who doesn't think rationally.

It's early morning, and as I walk by Ember's cottage, I sense she's still asleep—my ears picking up heavy breaths, imagining her chest rising and falling in her thin silk nightgown I've seen her in when she answers the door—when she's still not ready for work and I must wait for her to change before we begin our silent walk together through the forest.

I gave her the day off, but it infuriates me that she's able to sleep so soundly when I can barely find a minute of rest. I shake off my annoyance, realizing it's probably misguided. I'm not looking forward to this council meeting. It should be a joyous occasion with Red and Cameron welcoming their baby into the world, but Carmen had other plans.

I undress and place my folded clothes underneath a bush. I shift once I'm hidden in the tree line and sense my surroundings are clear, my paws meeting the forest floor. I race ahead, letting the crisp air running through my fur settle my nerves. The hidden council building comes into view. From the outside, it looks like an abandoned church—an old wooden building with vines crawling up all sides. It's deeper in the woods than the cave—or the office, as Ember knows it. We never share its location. The only way we can all find the building is that it's marked with our scent. Yes, we all piss on the side of the building. It's gross and undignified, but we are intelligent mythical dogs. We're going to be a little weird.

Only adults are allowed in this building, ensuring that no one catches us during our shift and reveals our identities, or those of the pack. We trickle into the building, not entering as a group. This makes things more inconspicuous, but also, we're nude once we're back in our human forms. My people aren't shy, but you can only take so much small talk when your dick is out.

Satisfied that I'm alone, I enter through the rickety door, stepping into the small entryway, a rack of heavy cloaks to my side and a frosted glass separating me from the main room. It's silent. I'm the first one here as always. Even my scattered mind won't allow me to abandon my punctuality.

I remove a black robe from a hanger and slip the heavy fabric over my shoulders before entering the meeting room. Light barely peeks through the board-ed-up windows, and empty wooden pews face a stage at the front. Soon they will be full of my pack—my people wearing matching robes. To an outsider, it may seem odd, but we're werewolves—the robes are the least weird thing about us. I can't help but wonder what Ember would think if she stumbled in on this meeting. I shake the image of her away as the first elderly member walks through the doors. I nod from the center stage as he enters. "Good morning, Roger. It's good to see you." He's a man of little words. He waves and takes his seat at the back of the room.

In less than twenty minutes, I've greeted every member who's walked through the door, and all seats are occupied. The crowd murmurs, already aware of what we're here to discuss. Sergeant Brick and Carmen are the last to enter, and all eyes flash to them as they make their way to the front of the room and sit in the first row. Carmen keeps her gaze on me, her expression never wavering. I know her well. Her hands clench at her side, even as her mate takes her hand and rubs his thumb over her skin. She's nervous—second-guessing her decision.

"Morning, family. It's good to see everyone well today." The crowd murmurs their agreement. "I won't draw this out. It's early. Most of us know why we're here. Carmen published a hundred-page exposé to the online Dayton Daily, going into detail to expose the Hunters for their crimes against us, not just the ones that are palatable for the public, specifically noting the experiments and the captured women that we rescued two weeks ago." The crowd is a mix of mumble reactions. I can tell some—the younger Weres—are excited that we're stepping out of the shadows and revealing the Hunters for who they truly are. And then the older generation—like me—fears for what this could mean. Our identities are compromised. Whether citizens choose to believe in the existence of Weres is a mystery, but what I know for sure is that the Hunters will strike back. It's just a matter of when.

I expect Carmen to butt in, to explain herself. She's always burned bright with her sense of justice—a trait I admire in her, even if this time I feel as if her pursuit is misguided. I glance at her, not wanting to put her on the spot, but only catch her downturned gaze.

I carry on. "Brick, any word from the DOS?" He clears his throat, releasing his mate's hand and addressing the room. "They're not happy, but so far, there's no immediate threat."

It's good to see them here, unified. Brick not only serves as the Sergeant for the Dayton Police Department, but also works for the Department of Supernatural. He recently went undercover as a double agent to keep an eye on the Hunters. He and Carmen discovered their local experiment facility, where the Hunters stored kidnapped Were-women and collected their menstruation to develop a serum that gave Hunters Were-powers. There's a long history of Hunters hating us but also wanting to obtain our abilities that they so loathe. Usually, this results in selective breeding for the cause—using the offspring as brainwashed soldiers—but it seems they grew tired of the unsavory task of procreating with our kind. Thankfully, we stopped this recent operation—or I should say, Carmen and Brick stopped it.

The pair have only been official for two weeks. I doubt Brick was aware that Carmen had released this exposé. It could potentially risk his job. But I suppose he's in the DOS's good graces since he just supplied them with such a big bust. It doesn't seem like Brick and Carmen are on the fritz due to this release. I don't want her to believe she can do whatever she wants without consulting the pack, but she's been through a lot. The two deserve to be happy above all else.

"Good." I nod to Brick, who takes his seat. I look back out to the crowd. "You all should read the article to arm yourself with the information that's available to the public." The tablet on my podium rings. I leave it here so the DOS can reach me in case of an emergency. Normally, a notification wouldn't draw my attention away from the task at hand, but the ping must mean something urgent.

I turn to the screen. Sure enough, it's addressed from the DOS but with a blank subject line. I click it open. It's a video of a press conference in DC. This isn't the place to look at this. I need to digest whatever is in front of me without the audience of my pack. Before I press play, I address the crowd. "Thank you all for being here, but I just got an urgent message I need to read."

"What is it?" someone says from the back of the room. The crowd sputters into rumblings.

"I'm not sure what it is yet, but the meeting is adjourned. As always, I will call a meeting if there is any immediate threat. If not, I will see you all next Wednesday."

The crowd rises to their feet, slowly exiting the building. Brick and Carmen approach. "What is it?" Carmen asks, her eyes full of panic.

"I don't know," I respond. "We'll watch it together."

We wait until the last pack member exits the building, taking far longer than usual to clear out the room. Probably because everyone's nosy and wants to hear what's going on for themselves. Finally, the three of us are alone. We share a glance before looking down and pressing play. Washington Senator Adam Green stands at the front of a large crowd, flags flanking him. Cameras and microphones sit in front of him, and he wears a grim expression. I recognize him. I never agreed with any of his policies. He's a wealthy businessman-turned-politician who seems more interested in growing his pockets than helping the average American citizen, but there was never any indication that he had a hand in the governmental dealings with werewolves and Hunters. Perhaps, he's just a spokesperson, perhaps more.

"I wanted to address the rumors of the existence of werewolves. Yesterday, an article was released detailing crimes committed by individuals in the name of stopping monsters—humans that transform into something else, unable to control themselves." My stomach drops, already knowing where this is heading. "The article was from a small paper, seemingly of little relevance, but I thought it was due time to bring the truth to the good people of America—to share what your government makes sure stays in the shadows and works toward eradicating for good." He turns toward the screen behind him and presses a button on the remote.

A blurry scene comes to life. It's a man, bloody and beaten, cornered at the edge of a cliff. Fangs flash as he snaps at the cameraperson, who stumbles backwards. His eyes glow golden, the same color as the setting sun at his back. There are more voices behind the camera, shouting and directing others—Hunters.

The man recognizes the camera, his panicked eyes flashing to the recorder, but as he nearly stumbles over the edge of a cliff, cornered, he has no other choice. He's not a novice with his abilities. The shift happens instantaneously. One second, he's a man, the next, he's a black wolf, large and powerful, jumping at his attacker. The camera falls to the ground, shaking before settling on the image of the werewolf, biting into the neck of a Hunter. It cuts off, right before blood bursts.

Carmen sobs as the focus returns to Senator Green. "America, that is a werewolf. A very real monster that lives amongst us. There aren't just a few but *packs* all around the country. We've done our best to shield you from the horrors and protect you without causing you alarm, but the time has come for the truth. They are speaking out, trying to make us humans seem like villains to attract more prey. We are the Hunters, but we can't defeat them on our own. We need every one of you to turn into Hunters and fight for the end of monsters."

I click pause. I've heard enough.

"Oh, my God. What have I done?" Carmen's voice shakes.

"This isn't your fault," Brick says, grabbing his mate's arm and bringing her into an embrace.

Although she broke the DOS's orders, I don't want her to take the blame. She was only doing what she thought was best for her people. "Let's calm down," I say. "We don't know how the public will receive this information. To me, it's clear from that video that the Hunters were trying to get the Were to attack."

Carmen sobs into Brick's chest.

I open a new window on my tablet and search for videos and forums relating to the press release. "Shit." I mean for it to be in my head, but it comes out loud. How can people react this quickly? Of course, there are naysayers, people who, just like me, don't trust Senator Green or what he stands for, let alone his recent claims. But most of the internet seems to be in agreement.

There are videos of people dressing up and searching the woods, self-proclaimed werewolf hunters. Forums detail their similar experience with us "monsters." Hate seems to be compounding upon itself from all corners of the world.

The Hunters have always been a threat, but this—every day people set on finding us and bringing an end to our kind—this is a shitstorm.

7

EMBER

How has it only been two weeks in this prison? Every day follows the same rhythm. Each morning, Grimm collects me at my cottage, walking me through the woods and to the dungeon he calls an office. He does his best to stay quiet during our treks, which you think would make me acutely aware of my surroundings, but for some reason, I never know how we got from point A to point B. He must take me on different routes each time. That or I'm studying his profile too acutely—his muscular build, the intricate design of the gray to dark brown of his hair.

I blame Stockholm syndrome, or maybe daddy issues. I don't want to be close to the man, but he's the only human I interact with day to day. Besides, I know there's something that he's not telling me about himself, and I'm waiting for him to crack.

I lounge in the rolling chair in my office. It's not even ten in the morning, and I'm already bored out of my fucking mind. Someone laughs far off in the distance, and my ears twitch, aching to hear life beyond my office. There are obviously other people working here, but they keep their distance from me. For all I know, Grimm could be playing a recording over a hidden intercom system in an attempt to make me feel not so isolated.

Today, he seemed more tense than usual. He didn't even say, "Good morning," like he usually does after I open my front door and step out onto the porch. I wanted to ask what was wrong, but I stopped myself. Every day should be miserable for him, and I don't need to look like I care. I just need human contact, or at least a change in scenery.

I stand, put my phone in my jeans pocket, and head toward the office door. I've got new plans for my usefulness. Grimm only gives me trivial tasks such as sorting notecards by color, organizing Excel files with emails, things I don't believe are pressing to his very obvious fake organization. I'm more and more confused about his point in keeping me here. I'm always waiting for the ball to drop, for Grimm to finally show his hand or take advantage of me. At this point, I welcome it.

I stick my head out of the office, making sure the coast is clear. He didn't say I wasn't allowed to leave, but he never showed me around the place, except the bathroom and the kitchen, which is surprisingly always stocked with something to eat right at lunchtime. I catch the glowing neon exit sign in the distance, taking a deep breath before rushing toward it without actively running.

When the doors shut behind me and the filtered sun through the canopy of leaves hits my face, I finally breathe out. I turn back toward the door, only finding the stone surface of the rock formation. I hope I can remember the combination of knocks Grimm uses to let us in every day. Damn it, why can't I remember anything when I'm in the presence of that man?

I take my phone out and hold it up to see if there's any signal. Is it possible to have negative bars? Perhaps they finally shut my phone off. I tried to cut all ties with my past, but I can't be without my phone. I know it's a risk. They could find me as long as my phone is near, but I doubt they care that much. Besides, what the fuck am I supposed to do without my phone?

Thankfully, I don't need phone service to capture videos and pictures. I twirl, recording the woods around me, playing with different angles, zooming in on the rock formation.

A hand grabs my shoulder, spinning me away from my shot. "What the fuck are you doing?" The voice hits like gravel to my eardrums. I swear, Grimm was clean-shaven this morning, but when I gaze up at him, stubble lines the cut of his jaw and runs down the side of his neck. His eyes seem to glow, and maybe it's my fright playing tricks on my mind, but fangs bulge under his tight lips.

It takes me a moment to wade through the fog of my fear, but once I do, I'm emboldened, pulling back from him and attempting to match his furious state. "I'm taking content." I step back, but he removes the distance, grabbing my hand that clutches my phone.

"What?" He's so close, his hot breath reaches my cheeks as he stares down at me.

My previous courage vanishes. He could really hurt me. We're alone in the woods, and there's something wrong about him, but I've always known that. My voice shakes. "I thought I could make a social media page to help promote the organization. You know, to help get more donations and recognition."

He presses forward, backing me into a tree. "I told you, we stay private. It's not safe."

"But how do you make money?" It's a legit question, but probably not the time to ask. He doesn't seem any closer to backing away from me, now pressed against me, not pinning me in place but making his nearness known.

"We're run by the government."

"Oh." It makes sense, but I know it's bullshit.

His hand braces himself against the tree, and he looks down at me with a heated stare. It takes me a moment to recognize there's something else there, not just anger but perhaps desire. What would I know about desire, though? Still, I can't help the way my stomach turns into heated coils, and my breath slows and quickens all at the same time. What the fuck is going on? My body betrays all reason, and my fingers ache to pull his neck to mine.

I close my eyes, unable to stare at him any longer. His breath grows heavier on my skin, and I swear he's moving closer to me. I know he's a monster and I should be terrified, but I can't take it anymore. I must know what he plans to do with me now that he has the chance.

He grunts, and I snap my eyes open, just in time to catch the shift of his expression. The hungry stare is gone, and in its place is a pointed repulsion. He pushes himself away from the tree and straightens his collar.

Shame washes over me before slowly turning into anger. I cross my arms in an attempt to mask my pain.

He clears his throat, unable to meet my eyes. "Well, now you know. No videos or pictures. No posting about us. Discretion is of the utmost importance. Especially now." He walks back to the "office," and when I don't follow, he whistles and motions forward. "Let's go. Inside."

I should refuse, demand more answers, or the freedom to at least come and go as I please, but my stupid feet pull me ahead to follow the monster who somehow now owns not only my time but my sanity.

8

GRIMM

I can't take it anymore—I've been driven to madness, to the monster they want me to become. No matter how tightly I shut my windows and doors, her smell permeates through my home. It's dark, only the full moon guiding my path as I stumble out of my front door, ripping my shirt off and foaming at the mouth. Images rush through my mind—her down-turned lips, the crease between her eyes. After everything I've done for her, she makes my life more miserable every day. It's not worth the risk to keep her so close. I know nothing about her. She could be like those people I saw on the internet, believing we're evil and should be destroyed. Perhaps not a Hunter, but now it seems that even an ordinary person could want our blood. She might not know who I am, but she hates me all the same. Good. It's been so long since I've tasted fresh flesh, and her fire might give her some added flavor.

I stumble across the green, trailing the lapping water of the lake. The crickets steady me, keeping me from completely shifting. I want her to know who's taking her—witness my full transformation before I devour her. I swing her cottage door open, or should I say *my* cottage door. Everything on this property is mine—even her. I own her, and it's due time she pays up. I tumble through the doorway, led by her scent growing ever more powerful. When I burst through the bedroom door, her eyes are already on me, wide as I remember them. She pulls the sheet to her chest, her white skin even paler in the moonlight from her window.

I slow my steps. She's clearly frightened by my entering, and if I make any sudden movements, she might attempt to flee, and I'll miss the chance to get her right where I want her. She's been rotten since the day I laid eyes on her, but now she makes up for it. She waits for me, breath heavy as if anticipating my attack. Just how I like it, the room misty with her scent.

I'm barely able to hold my shift back as I approach the edge of her bed, her lips part around strained breaths that seem to fill my lungs with the oxygen they'd need for a proper feast. The mattress melts under my knees as I crawl to her, anticipating her fight. She continues to surprise me. Instead of screaming and kicking me away, she lowers the sheet, revealing her pebbled chest poking through the thin material of her nightgown. Has she been waiting for me? Her skin flushes, but not with fear, but perhaps desire. No, it can't be, it must be my aching cock playing tricks on me. She hates me, has made it more than apparent since I've captured her. This must be a ruse to lure me to her trap, to my demise.

I welcome the challenge, and as I crawl closer, she falls to her back. I move over her, so close that I can almost taste her. I wait for her surprise attack, certain she has plans for me. She may be young and naive, but her eyes hold the cunning of a fox. Perhaps that's why I've been so drawn to her, eager to discover her angle in all of this.

Her hands rest above her head, her silver hair flowing around her like starlight. I've been curious about the shade. It can't be natural, although her roots seem to be the same color as the rest of her strands. Another point to my speculation that she's not what she seems, clearly not as unfortunate as she plays.

Seconds tick by, perched over her as our breaths grow thicker, mixing into each others'. I barely notice my claws piercing into the mattress or the coarse hair running down my neck and arms. She must know what I am, but she doesn't question; her eyes only swim with desire. Her chest arches into me, and her eyelids droop slightly. I can't take it anymore. I crash against her, tasting the plush cushions of her lips.

She opens her mouth, welcoming my exploring tongue, my fangs just pricking above her lips. She tastes so much sweeter than I could imagine, and as I run my hand up the silk of her garment, stopping once I reach her peak. I'm sure I'll burst just from the feel of her. She moans into my mouth, pushing into my hand, wanting more.

Perhaps she'll be my demise, because as she offers herself, I have no reserve to hold back. I planned to sneak into her room and ruin her, but I never antici-pated it would be so welcomed.

She spreads for me, her legs vining around my mid-dle and grinding me into her. I grunt, so close to my release, but the urge to knot inside of her overtakes me. Except that's impossible. I don't knot. I'm not the kind of Were that breeds any female he enters. There's only one. Still the urge feels the same. I want to rip her in two, claim her as completely mine.

She bucks against me, and I almost pull back so as not to lose myself completely. Her wetness permeates through my shorts. She's bare. Ready for the taking. I look down as I pull myself free, my cock hard and already leaking from my tip.

When I return my eyes to hers, ready to mark my claim, she's anew. Gone is the malleable angel splayed before me. In her place lies a hardened woman, ha-tred burning in her eyes. Her hands clasp around a sharpened knife, and I barely have a second before she lunges for me, piercing me through my heart.

I jolt up from bed, clutching my chest and gulping air as if I'm a beached fish. "What the fuck?" I mutter. The dark room around me slowly comes into view, calming me. It was just a dream. I'm sweating, completely bare except for my tented shorts. I press down on my full mast, embarrassed even if no one else is here to witness my shame. At least I didn't finish on myself, but the pressure building deep in my abdomen tells me I was mere seconds away from doing so. Perhaps I'm going through a male form of menopause. First, I'm unable to control my shifts, now my dreams seem more real than fiction, and I wake myself with morning wood like a pup going through puberty. Except it's not the morning, still the middle of the night, but there's no chance of returning to sleep.

I contemplate my dream, remembering the uncontrolled urge to have her on my lips, then my desire, just to end with a knife through my heart. I deserved to die at the end of it, even my subconscious knows it. How could I think such evil thoughts? Perhaps I am a monster when I don't hold myself back. It was just a dream, but it all felt so real.

I jump to my feet, unable to contemplate my tangled strings of emotions any longer. My large house has never felt smaller, and I push myself out through the kitchen door, the still night air immediately calming my nerves.

I fall to the wooden porch floor, breathing in the cool air, trying my best to focus on anything else but her. This is all her fault. Sure, I wasn't in my prime before her arrival, the stress of leading on my own was gradually wearing on me, but I wasn't this—a deranged animal. It's all too much, the stress piling up on itself.

I need to let her go, get her out of my life for good. Fuck the damn sports car. I need an actual assistant—a werewolf assistant that won't jeopardize the safety of our pack. She was trying to film our location, for Christ's sake. She's a fucking liability and a distraction. Whatever has made me keep her around for this long doesn't matter anymore. In the morning, I'll send her on her way. I'll get her a bus ticket and give her a month's pay. I'll be done and focused.

Somehow, my plan doesn't make me as relieved as I'd like. I decide a sweat session might be enough to clear my head and allow me to return to bed. I do a quick thirty sit-ups before flipping over for fifty push-ups. The night air has cooled me off some, but my internal body temperature still rages from my dream. Sweat drips down my temple in mere minutes.

I jump to my feet, reaching for the pull-up bar at the top of the porch frame. The workout has been good for me, but as my muscles strain under my reps, I notice that the guest house lights are on. Ember's silhouette walks across the porch and down the steps, heading toward the base of the lake.

I halt, dropping to my feet as I study her. What is she doing up so late? I don't think she can see me since my house isn't lit up, but I still hide most of myself behind a pillar as I watch her. She walks further into the water, her ankles covered before reaching down and pulling off her dress, throwing it to a rock behind. My breath gets stuck in my throat.

I shift my eyes, able to make her out through the darkness. I don't even register that I do it. It happens like second nature, and I'm relieved to find her wearing undergarments as she drops into the water. I'd kill myself if she were naked and I was the old creep watching her from his porch. I'm still a creep, but this is somewhat better.

I can't help but wonder if she awoke from her own unsettling dreams. Perhaps some involving a monster like me. No, that's preposterous. I can't even entertain the idea. This is precisely why I need to let her go tomorrow.

A splash startles me as she dives completely into the water. The moonlight glints atop the ripples of water as she pushes herself out farther toward the center. Ember is beautiful, there's no doubt about it, but there's nothing graceful in the way she moves through the water. It's not until she doesn't move any further but instead dunks below the surface, her hands grasping for an imaginary lifeline that I realize what's happening. She's drowning.

There are no thoughts, only instinct. I shift and run to rescue her.

9

EMBER

My consciousness sparks like fireflies, slowly fading out as the day approaches. Breath inflates my lungs, and I roll to the side to vomit the water taking up too much space. I cough, my awareness returning as I'm pulled into the air, cradled by strong arms. I keep my eyes closed, the pain in my chest and my head too great to do anything but lie helplessly.

A door swings open, followed by heavy footsteps, before I'm placed on a soft surface. It's quiet now, and I register the difference from the noisy night. I open my eyes, examining my room around me. It takes me a few moments to make out the man approaching me, pushing two fingers to my neck, and then touching a spot on my calf. Pain shoots through me. I cry out, bending forward, my heart racing, and I'm finally awake.

"What the fuck?" I yell, pushing Grimm away, who I can only assume is the perpetrator of my pain. I catch my bloodied shin.

"I'm trying to clean your wound. Lie down." He lifts a white piece of fabric.

I follow his orders, lying on my back and pushing wet strands of hair out of my face. "What happened to my leg?"

"I think you hit it on a rock or a branch when you were drowning." Memories come back to me—my body heavy in the dark water, the black liquid filling my lungs, the panic, the pain, and then nothing. I breathe heavily, the memories too close for comfort.

Grimm grabs my arm, rubbing his thumb across my flesh. "Calm down. You're okay now." He continues to dab my wound, and I hiss at the sting.

"It's alcohol, so that it won't get infected."

The pain slowly subsides, and I let my wet body melt into my sheets, focusing on regulating my breath.

Grimm's presence has never brought me comfort, but as he wraps my leg with gauze and rechecks my pulse, I'm at peace. I've never had someone tend to me like this. Perhaps this is what it feels like to have a caring father, but that thought quickly vanishes when I catch his bare chest and his athletic shorts molding to his sculpted thighs, all of him still dripping with water. I don't view him as a father, not even close.

He sits at the edge of my bed, farther away from me than I'd like, but his hand rests on my ankle, rubbing his thumb back and forth. The touch is so light, yet all my awareness in my body travels to that point. His eyes hold mine, and I can't help the quickening of my heart or the heaviness of my chest. Is this what it's like to be touched by him? To hold his soft gaze? I find myself lost in all of this, eager for more.

He seems in a similar trance, leaning forward slightly but stopping and shaking his head. "You shouldn't swim by yourself so late. You're lucky I was there."

He's right, of course, but the moment clears. Resentment pushes away the longing. "I didn't want anyone to watch me for my first time."

He straightens, his eyes creasing. "You mean the first time in that lake?"

"Yeah, but also my first time ever."

"You don't know how to swim?"

"Doesn't everyone know how to swim?"

He pops to his feet. "What do you mean? You have to learn how to swim. Surely you know that."

Suddenly, I'm embarrassed. Which is preposterous since I also realize I'm not wearing clothes except my black bra and underwear. Seems like my shame should have arrived much earlier. I grab my blanket and pull it to my chest—entirely too self-conscious of everything. "I know," I lie.

"So you decided to learn how to swim for the first time in your life, by yourself in the middle of the night?"

"Obviously!" I yell, rage boiling over. My mind clouds, and panic takes hold. I don't want him to know the truth about my upbringing, and I'm worried my apparent ignorance will reveal too much.

Grimm's eyes trail to the top of my head, growing in surprise. I didn't even notice the change, but I feel it now that his attention is on the spot. I run my fingers through my hair, pretending I'm just fixing myself instead of hiding. "Well, thanks for saving me or whatever, but you can leave now." I cross my arms over my chest, painfully aware of the sheet that has fallen to my lap.

He stands, clearing his throat. "Yeah, you're welcome." He walks toward the door, but stops, hugging the doorframe. "If you want to learn, I'd be happy to teach you."

"Teach me?"

"To swim."

I study him, alarmed by the sincerity of his voice, the shake of his eyes as if nervous.

"Oh, right." He stares at me a moment longer; it's intense and overwhelming, but finally it ends. He nods and exits the room.

I'm left alone, wet, and confused. He didn't have to save me. Of course, a girl dying in his lake would be rather annoying, but perhaps he's not the monster I've imagined.

This doesn't change anything, though. Be damned, my pounding heart. My mission remains the same.

10

GRIMM

I barely slept a wink last night. If I thought my cock ached when I woke up from my startling dream, after being so close to Ember and having her wet body in my arms, my manhood was a steel rod of agony. Of course, when I brought my lips to hers and gave her CPR, I only thought about helping her, making sure she was okay. I'd never imagined I would be so worried for her safety, but seeing her unconscious on the shore as I pressed against her chest, breathing air into her lungs—it was torture. After I placed her in her bed and knew she was okay, the fire I felt before her rescue reflamed.

I tried to resist. It's not appropriate to jack off at the thought of an employee, especially one who is twenty years my junior, but I couldn't take it anymore. I rushed to the bathroom, lathered my hand in the unscented lotion under my sink, and tugged my cock until I erupted, my cum so thick and plentiful that I wasn't sure it would stop flowing from my tip.

Of course, with my relief came self-loathing, but it didn't last long. It seemed all I needed was that release to fall back to sleep. It startled me to wake to the morning sun piercing through my open window. Dreams didn't torment me like usual. Perhaps taking myself in hand would be the remedy for my mental afflictions, except when I began my day, my body already humming with the anticipation of being near Ember again, it was apparent that the self-pleasure was a temporary fix. Perhaps only stoking the flame.

When I picked her up this morning, allowing her a few hours to sleep in, she seemed well enough. Less hatred in her eyes, but maybe I'm just imagining that. If anything, she appeared meek, unable to meet my eyes, and didn't try to stir up my anger to remove the silence like she usually does.

I wanted to bring up what happened. Not just the near-death experience she endured, but also what I witnessed. It's obviously not something she wants to discuss. She must not have any idea who I am, because she seemed ashamed of herself.

I really need to teach her how to get to the office. I'm purposely distracting her, taking her a different route every time. In fact, it's located much closer than she believes. We circle it twice before I lead her to the entrance. I continue to blame my misdirection on my skepticism of her, but today, when I imagined telling her the truth, I realized it might be something else that's driving me to spend more time with her. Perhaps I still don't trust her, but after last night, it's more dangerous to spend time with her alone than to reveal secrets of our pack.

I was supposed to let her go today, but it doesn't feel like the right time. Maybe she doesn't have to go if what I suspect is true. One thing is sure: something needs to change between us. If we continue on like this, I'll never get any work done, and today requires my attention.

I'd usually welcome a distraction to my confusing thoughts, but unfortunately, the emails and videos littering my monitor make me want to think of anything else. These aren't things I can just shove away, though. They require me to take action. What that action is, however, I'm not sure.

The DOS is up my ass. I'm not the only werewolf Minister in North America, but since the start of the recent war came from my pack, they seem to think I also need to come up with the solution. Not to mention that the more recent werewolf-sighting videos leaked online seem to be coming from Dayton. It's not apparent, but I can tell from the foliage. I know my home well, and there's someone here who is set on revealing our pack.

Carmen has already been in today. Her previous shame and regret in her exposé have transformed into a fiery desire to end what she started. I've tasked her with patrolling the woods and hidden homes of the members of our pack to keep her busy. That's about the only thing any of us can do right now.

I click on the last link in the never-ending list recently sent to me by the DOS. It's another press conference from the White House. Senator Green stands before a crowd of reporters. "Senator, what is your response to the civilians attempting to hunt the monsters on their own?" asks a woman from the crowd.

"Great question. I encourage any able-bodied men to go after the beasts if you know of any nearby. I've also heard of individuals traveling to places like Dayton, Washington, where a powerful pack is located. Be wary, protect yourself and your loved ones, but I commend you in your drive for justice."

I turn it off. "Jesus fucking Christ." So it's no coincidence that the new videos that surfaced are from our neck of the woods. Senator Green sent people here. That exposé must have really pissed him off.

Someone knocks on my door. "Come in," I call, removing my feet from the corner of my desk.

Cameron enters my office.

"What are you doing here?" I ask. "You should be home with Red and the baby." My stomach drops. It must be urgent if he felt the need to come here himself.

"We caught Hunters."

"Hunters?"

"Well, wanna-be Hunters. They're inexperienced. They were sneaking around my property and poking their cell phones into the cracks of my windows. There was a group of three. I've already gone through their phones and found all the evidence I need to confirm they were looking to catch one of us shifting. They weren't just there to expose us, though. They had weapons."

I catch the simmer of rage behind his eyes. "Are they alive?"

"Yes, we have them locked up in the dungeons. It's your call what we do with them."

I'm baffled but relieved. Any other male Were would have slaughtered the perpetrators, especially one with a newborn child and a bedbound mate. It's either because this is precisely what Cameron has been trained for his whole life—being hunted—or he must have realized how bad it would look for us if the media discovered these "Hunters" murders.

"Take me to them." I follow him out of my office, unable to stop the first thought in my mind. I hope Ember can't hear what we've discussed. I don't want the moment she discovers the truth about us to be when we've captured human prisoners.

We walk through the winding hallways. Luckily for my attempts to keep Ember in the dark, the dungeons are on the other side of the building. Water drips in the distance, and the lights lower. If we're going to refer to our holding cells as a "dungeon," we want it to appear as such. This building is over a hundred years old, and although we've updated the office spaces, it seemed fitting to keep most of it in the original design. Besides, if the Hunters already think we're archaic beasts, we might as well put on a show for them.

Before we step into the hall leading to the cells, we reach a coat room with hanging black cloaks. I pull the dark fabric over myself and flip up the hood. "Did they see anyone else?" I ask.

"No, I blindfolded them after I captured them and called Reggie to help me transport them here." Cameron's strengths have always impressed me. It's why he's been chosen since he was a young child to be the Human Liaison—the most powerful who can withstand the dangers that come with his identity being public knowledge. But even now, I'm speechless that he was able to overpower three grown men on his own. I study him, amazed.

He reads me well. He clears his throat and shakes his head. "Like I said, they were inexperienced, plus Red helped me contain them."

I remove my hood. "Is she okay?" My body sits on pins and needles.

"Of course. They'd be dead if she weren't. Besides, she's powerful, able to control people's minds without even touching them, remember?" He taps my forehead. "Don't doubt her just because she had a baby."

"Of course. I'm sorry. For all of this. It's ridiculous." I follow him down the long, dark corridor. He said that the prisoners were blindfolded, but I still keep my cloak on.

"Don't blame yourself." He turns to look at me as we walk through the wooden door. "Blame my troublesome sister."

"You can't blame her," I whisper, growing closer to the dungeons.

He laughs. "It *is* her fault, no doubt, but I know why she did it. Just wish she had waited a little farther away from the birth of my daughter." I study his profile as we approach the cells. His eyes are bagged, his smile lines deepen, and the low light picks up a sprinkling of grays. Perhaps I'm not the only tortured mind.

"Let us go!" A red-faced man squawks as I'm mere inches away from the bars.

"Why should we?" I respond, holding back my rage. "It seems like you were trying to murder one of our own."

The greasy-haired blond next to him speaks up. "We weren't going to hurt anyone. The weapons were just for our protection. All we wanted was evidence of the werewolves to go viral online."

I examine the three men beneath my hood, shaking behind their blindfolds, the fronts of their pants soiled. I wait as long as I can, wanting them to stew in my silence, to take years off their pitiful lives with worry. Finally, I clear my throat. "Call Brick. Have him arrest them for trespassing. Destroy their phones."

Cameron hides a grimace, taking a moment to answer. A part of me wanted to end these bastards—the piece undoubtedly larger in Cameron, but we must keep our humanity. We must do what's right for our people. "You got it, boss," he finally responds.

I turn away, unable to ponder my decision much longer. My pulse races with fury as I make my way back to my office, needing a second to breathe, needing a distraction. I've spent my whole life in this building, my father, the werewolf Minister, before me. I could navigate its corridors with my eyes closed, my senses barred. Yet even with my familiarity, my feet work on their own, bringing me to the one place I truly want to be.

I swing open Ember's office door. She's sitting on the floor in front of her desk, scrolling through her phone. Her eyes catch mine in surprise.

"Do you want to go to lunch with me in town?" I ask.

Her lips part. She studies me, words seemingly lost in her throat. She shakes her head and answers, "Yeah, sure," before rising to her feet.

It's just two words, but somehow, I'm already lighter.

11

EMBER

As quaint, picturesque downtown Dayton comes into view, I'm filled with annoyance. It's been weeks, and this is my first experience of civilization. I lean against Grimm's passenger window, sulking, reminded that I'm his prisoner, regardless of my body's stupid reaction to the sincere look in his eyes when he asked me to lunch.

Grimm clears his throat, turning down the radio playing '80s hits. "You know, you can always take my car and drive into town if you'd like."

His words startle me, and I straighten, certain he must have read my mind. "Oh yeah? I thought I wasn't allowed to leave." I don't hide the venom in my words.

He rolls his eyes, and it's honestly relieving to see him back to himself. Ever since he saved my life, or whatever, the night before, he's been different—almost bashful. "You're not my prisoner, Ember. You work for me."

"So I'm *just* your employee then?"

He takes his eyes off the road, examining me, something flashing across his stare. I didn't mean for my words to be suggestive, but now that they're out and only silence follows, I can't help the heating of my blood. I whip my attention back to the road as Grimm clears his throat.

"Where are we going exactly?" I ask, crossing my arms over my chest. I'm not sure why I keep acting like a moody teenager.

"Joanne's Diner," he replies. "I've gotten you food from there before."

I wasn't aware he got food specifically for me. Besides the bags of groceries that show up at my door, I thought the meals constantly stocked in the office kitchen were for everyone. However, I suppose I never see anyone working on our side of the office, so that makes sense. I don't know why it warms the icy corners of my heart that he goes out to get me something besides a cold sandwich I could assemble myself. He made me write a list of what I usually eat and my preferences on my second day, but I don't consider that a kind gesture. I'm not much of a prisoner if I'm starved.

I take in the groups of people as we slowly drive by. For such a small and desolate town on the outskirts, downtown seems to be quite populous. Families chat with passersby, children scampering around their ankles. Groups of young women laugh, holding cardboard cups of coffee. Old men sit on benches, seeming to complain about one thing or another to each other. Of course, DC had this sort of thing—communities with interconnected lives—it was just something I was never part of.

"Yes, right up front!" Grimm cheers, his face lighting up into a boyish grin as he pulls into a spot in front of his mentioned diner. I hate that his reaction is so charming.

He parks the car, racing out and opening the door for me. He's old, probably beaten by nuns if he didn't offer this gentlemanly gesture while growing up, but I can't help the flutters in my stomach as I step out on the sidewalk. I don't thank him. I don't want him to think I'm starting to like him or anything, because I most definitely am not. Definitely not.

I follow him into the restaurant, and of course, he holds the door for me as we enter. The bell above the door chimes, and a waitress tells us to pick any booth.

"Wow, it's just like the movies," I say, mostly to myself as we slide into the sticky red booth nearest the door.

The waitress, a gray-haired woman wearing a light blue apron, follows us and drops off our menus. Grimm picks it up but addresses me. "You've never been to a diner before?"

Shit. This must be like swimming, something normal people are supposed to experience before they're twenty years old. "Not one like this," I lie, turning my attention to the sticky, laminated menu. I can feel Grimm's gaze on me as I scan.

The waitress comes back ridiculously quickly. "What can I get ya?" she asks, smacking her gum and placing ice waters in front of us. I panic, glancing over the string of words before me.

"I'll have the breakfast sampler and she'll have the short stack with a side of bacon."

I'm relieved by the absence of my decision, which isn't surprising since it's what I'm used to, but I can't help but wonder how he knew what I'd want. I scrunch my lips, handing the waitress the menu back.

"What if I hate bacon?" I ask, placing my folded arms on the table.

"Then it would be strange that you mentioned it as one of your preferred grocery items." He swirls the ice in his cup before taking a big chug, downing nearly half of it. I can't help that I watch the bob of his Adam's apple, the sight oddly exciting.

"Grimm," someone says excitedly from behind me. I turn to find a stunningly beautiful redheaded woman walking through the door. Something like jealousy sparks, but obviously, it can't be that.

Grimm stands, rushing toward her. "Red, what are you doing here? You look great," he says as he wraps her into a bear hug. I recognize the name. This must be Cameron's wife.

A brunette with a nose ring enters, a car seat hanging from her arm. She doesn't seem as excited to see Grimm. Neither of them notices me. Why would they?

"Carmen," Grimm says, acknowledging the woman, his smile less brilliant. "And is this the special lady?" he asks, already kneeling to look beneath the visor. "Oh, my God, Red, she's beautiful," he says, hovering in a squat. I watch this all play out, turned around in my booth. I'm eager to see the baby myself, because from the look on Grimm's face, she truly must be the most beautiful thing to ever exist. Fuck my woman biology that swoons at this intimidating man turning into mush at the sight of an infant.

Red sighs. "She's definitely cute, but she hates to sleep. Carmen thought it would be a good idea to get out of the house for a little bit."

"Cameron called me and asked to stay with her for a little while," Carmen says, addressing Grimm, her eyes serious.

A tall man enters, placing a hand on the small of Carmen's back. Grimm straightens, his face void of all previous wonder. "Brick? What are you doing here?"

"Don't worry. I've got my best men taking care of them. We'll get them charged with as much as we can."

Grimm's chest deflates. "Okay, good."

Brick steps closer, lowering his voice, but not enough for me to miss his words. "We're calling in more support from the DOS. We'll have more men patrolling. I'm sorry about this, boss, but we'll do our best to keep everyone safe."

Grimm nods, tight-lipped, before shooting his eyes to me—swiveled in the booth next to them, arms under my chin. He clears his throat, tensing at the realization that I'm here, close enough to hear his safe-guarded secrets. "Everyone, I'd like to introduce you to Ember, my new secretary."

The trio studies me, their expressions unrevealing for a moment until Red cracks a smile, looking from me to Grimm. "Ah, yes. Cameron told me about your new secretary. Nice to meet you, Ember. I'm Red."

I prop myself up to my knees, making myself taller so I can meet her at eye level with the back of the booth in between us. "Nice to meet you," I reply, taking her hand.

"How are you liking the new gig?" Carmen asks, switching the car seat to the other hand.

I shrug, unsure how to react with so many eyes on me. "Didn't really have a choice." I don't have to look at Grimm to know how he'll react to my words. It's like I can feel the stiffening of his bones.

To confirm my suspicion, he clears his throat, his throat strained. "Of course you have a choice, Ember."

Feeling brazen, I shoot him a glare. "Oh, really?"

"Of course."

For a moment, there's only the two of us, staring down each other to see who will break first. It's not until Red clears her throat that I remember we are not alone and an entire diner is around us. "We'll let you two get back to your lunch. It seems you have a lot to discuss."

Grimm shakes out of it, stepping closer to me, but addresses the group. "Right. Well, it was great to see you all and especially the newest addition." He leans down, waving a finger at the tiny baby with a giddy smile. Carmen turns the car seat toward us, and I finally get a chance to see the sleeping bundle. She's really cute. I can tell, even though I haven't seen many babies in real life. I can't help the smile straining my cheeks. Maybe there's a reason people choose to endure the pain of childbirth if something as cute as that comes out.

"Nice to meet you, Ember," Red says. "If you need anything, have Grimm give you my number."

"Will do." I give her an obviously forced smile. She seems nice enough and has a cute baby, but I still don't trust any of them.

"Bye, Ember," Carmen says as she follows Red to a booth at the other end of the diner. Brick nods and smiles at me before giving Grimm an odd look—almost sympathetic, knowing. It's annoying.

Grimm slides back into the other side of the booth, taking a sip of his water. I turn to him, my arms over my chest. "So, what was that about?"

"What?"

"What Brick mentioned, *charging them with as much as they can?*"

The server comes back, two enormous, steaming plates in her hands. She places the impossibly large stack of pancakes with the side of bacon in front of me and the other, filled with eggs, hash browns, sausage, and bacon, in front of Grimm. It sketches me out that the food arrived so fast. Nothing worth eating should come out of the kitchen that quickly, but as I cut a small section of the stack and take a skeptical bite, the fluffy deliciousness surprises me. I moan around the bite, shutting my eyes. These are nothing like the pancakes I attempt to make myself in Grimm's guest house.

I remember myself—the image I'm supposed to be portraying. I turn my attention to the man before me. He eyes me, in the way he should be looking at his meal. I turn away, the thing between us too heavy to hold. He shakes his head. "You don't need to worry about that," he says, steering the conversation back on track.

"Above my pay grade?" I ask before wrapping my lips around my straw.

"Something like that." He stuffs his mouth with eggs.

"When are you going to tell me what it is we *really* do at the 'office?'"

"When are you going to tell me the truth about you?"

My insides squeeze. "What are you talking about?"

He scrapes his fork against his plate, just adding height to my nerves. "I'll be honest when you're honest?" He smirks, as if this is all a joke. How could he know? And why call me out now? Unless he means something else. It must be that because he's too casual. I hope I'm masking my panic in case he's just referring to the time theft I've been committing in the office or the dreams about a certain man that wake me in a sweat.

"It's always games with you," I say before shoving as much pancake into my mouth as possible. I want this to be over. I want to be in my small cottage overlooking the lake and away from this man.

"I could say the same thing about you."

I push my plate away. "I'm only here because of you. I don't want to play games. I want to be away from all of this."

He snaps. "There it is."

"There what is?"

"I can tell when you're lying."

I stand, making more noise than I'd like. "I'm done. I'll wait in the car." I walk out of the restaurant, catching Red staring at me from her booth.

As I pull myself into the pickup truck, I contemplate if I should just run away. What if he does know the truth? It could mean danger for me. But all my belongings are in the cottage, and I can't make the call to go back to where I came from. I would rather take my chances with this monster than that.

It's not even five minutes before Grimm angrily enters the truck. I don't look at him, even though it's a stupid decision. I should be examining him, reading him to gauge his next move. He doesn't say anything to me, just pulls out and heads down the road we came from.

I keep my eyes on the old buildings as we pass. Once we're at the stoplight before the exit from downtown, with only trees as far as the eye can see ahead of us, I notice commotion at the far end of the last building, almost in the shadows, but not enough to miss. Grimm puts the car into park. I turn to him just as he hops out. "What are you doing?" I ask, but it's too late, he's already charging at the two men cornering a woman pressed up against the gray wall. I follow after him, instinct taking over reason.

"What's going on here?" he yells, nearing closer. "Mary, are you alright?"

"Grimm!" The young woman shouts back.

The light-haired man presses up against her, intimidating her in an attempt to quiet her. It works, and she cowers, her hands opening and closing.

The dark-haired man points his phone at the two as he addresses Grimm. "I know what it looks like, but this woman is a monster. We saw her change into one of those werewolves everyone is talking about in the woods the night before. I can show you the video."

It happens so fast. Grimm grabs the man's phone, smashing it in his hand as if it's made of a thin plastic instead of metal and glass. It shouldn't be possible for a human man, but of course...

"What the fuck?" yells the owner of the phone. "You're one of them, aren't you?"

Grimm steps closer, changing right before my eyes. His shirt splits at the center of his back, dark fur bursting through. His hands grow, sharp nails poking from his fingertips. I can't see his face, but the man he's cornering can't tear his eyes away from it, terror flashing across his features.

"Mary, go," Grimm directs the woman without looking at her, stepping closer to the man before him. The woman doesn't hesitate, slipping away from the other man who is too interested in Grimm to notice, and running through the woods behind the buildings. I can't catch to see if she shifted as well, but she's gone quickly.

Despite the dark-haired man's terrified demeanor, he's not as meek as he seems. He whips a gun from his pocket, aiming it at Grimm's head. Until this moment, I'm a bystander, watching the dramatic turn of events, but as Grimm's tall shoulders turn down, something snaps within me. "Step back!" the man shouts, his voice shaking. Grimm heeds his request, but I don't.

It's never happened like this before, not being able to control my change. Of course, that's not true. As a child, I was dangerous, but I was trained, kept hidden, and learned to suppress the natural instincts within me.

Now it's as if I'm acting outside of my body. I blink, and I'm between Grimm and the man with the pistol. He seems just as startled as I am. I'm just there—my bushy tail raised behind me, my ears straight, and my eyes burning as if their bright hue is in full force. I can't do much. This version of myself isn't as powerful as it is disturbing, but it's all Grimm needs.

He grabs the gun, now pointed away from us and raised to the side since the man isn't focused on Grimm anymore. He doesn't give up without a fight, though, pulling the trigger as Grimm's hand wraps around his.

I scream, ducking away from the men. Luckily, the bullet fires away from all of us. Grimm overpowers the man as easily as if he were a toddler, bringing him down to the ground and smashing his gun-wielding hand. He pockets the pistol, not taking his weight off him.

The other man runs off into the woods. Grimm may expect me to chase him, but why would I do that? Why did I even do *anything?* Except I know the reason.

"Ember, grab my phone in the truck and call Brick," Grimm orders, still restraining the man to the ground with his body weight.

It startles me out of my stupor, and I race toward the vehicle. Of course, it's the obvious first response from him, but I can't help my surprise. I revealed my monster, and Grimm isn't repulsed. That's a first.

12

GRIMM

It's fitting that the sky opens up, washing the world as we drive down the winding roads, away from downtown and back home. Water falls from Ember's eyes as well, and all I want to do is figure out why. It could be the obvious reason: Ember just witnessed violence. Those men could have killed someone, and if she didn't intervene as she did, it would likely be me. She doesn't seem like the type of person who would take many life-risking actions. She's obviously lived a sheltered life, one I'm still uncertain is something normal.

Or, she could be upset because she shifted, a secret she's clearly been told to hide. It puzzles me why she would be upset by this, though. I revealed myself to her as well—not completely, but she'd have to be blind not to realize I'm a werewolf.

I try to remain quiet, even as I glance at her from the corner of my eye every five seconds. If she wants to discuss what happened, she will. Except, I can't sit by while I watch her break in front of me. I want to stop driving, pull her into my arms, and run my hand down her silky hair until she calms. Obviously, that's not an option, so instead, I open my big mouth. "You did well back there."

Her sobbing stops momentarily. "What?"

"If you hadn't shifted and intervened, I'd be dead."

She cries harder. Damn, maybe she wishes I died.

I turn down the trail to my house, unmarked but obvious to me. "What I'm trying to say is, you should be proud of yourself, your abilities."

"Abilities?" She scoffs. "That part of myself is disgusting, nothing to be proud of."

She pulls her knees up and folds into herself. I put the car in park as we reach the beginning of my long driveway, reaching over and placing my hand on her back. "Why would you say that?"

She pops her head up; her large eyes are red and glassy. "I'm a monster."

I cup her chin. I'm unsure if it's the cold rain tucking us in, or just watching her so distraught, I can't help but touch her. "I don't think you're a monster." It's an obvious response. We're the same, even if our Were-forms seem to be different species. She didn't complete the shift, just revealing a bushy, red tail and small, pointed ears coming from the crown of her head. If I had to guess I'd say she's a werefox. There are many different variations of Weres, such as Brick, who is a werepig. They're less common than werewolves, but it's not surprising to come across them.

The look on her face is one of shock, as if she can't believe what I'm saying. She doesn't respond, though, only tracks my face as if she wants more from me, as if she craves validation she's never received.

I answer her silent request. "Ember, you were born this way, but it's up to you how you wield your power. You saved people today because of your abilities. You're special, chosen for more."

I barely notice she's moved forward, but her smell thickens, and I'm able to examine more of her fine features. "But I can't always control it. I'm dangerous."

"Have you practiced using your abilities?"

She shakes her head in my hand.

"That's all you need. It's just like when you're a teenager and you have these urges that you feel like you can't contain, but with time, you grow into yourself and learn how to sate the desires and turn on your abilities when you want to." I don't mean to sound suggestive, talking about puberty urges and such, but from the way Ember's lips part in my hands, it seems as if this fog coming over us isn't just from my end.

I'm lying to her. I talk about training and how, with practice, nothing can make us uncontrollable, but that's not the truth. Something about her makes me lose my control—whether it be through anger or the rushing blood down my body—she makes me the beast I've previously kept in check.

Right now, it is no different. She's vulnerable, ignorant of the world and herself—it's not the time to inch forward. Her eyelids drop as the distance evaporates between us, and I'm leaning more over the middle console. It's clear she wants me on her lips, but this isn't the time. This isn't right. But morality can't break through my desire, no matter how hard the rational side of me tries.

I can't take it anymore, breaking the rhythm of our slow ascension and crashing my lips against hers. She parts for me, welcoming my searching tongue, and I greedily take what's given. I need her closer, the taste of her only heightening my need. I grab the back of her neck and pull her harder against me. The stupid middle console makes me want to tear my truck apart piece by piece, and she would be the culprit of both of my vehicles turning to ruin.

She rises to her knees, her hands running through my hair and down my neck, making me tilt my head upwards so our contact doesn't break. She's about to climb into my lap. I moan into her mouth, anticipating her weight on my hardened length. It's been too long, and I'm terrified I'm about to embarrass myself. But then something shifts. She breaks away from our contact, her eyes searching me in horror. She pushes herself away.

"Ember," I call, my voice as pained as my body.

She doesn't turn, but yanks open the passenger door, throwing herself into the wash of rain and taking off to her cottage.

I'm left alone, my breath still heavy, my cock still throbbing, and an overwhelming feeling of shame. Of course, this isn't what she wants. She's a beautiful young woman. I'm an old creep. Despite what I felt and her reaction to my embrace, a large part of her knows this can never be.

I'm a monster, doing no good to prove how special she really is.

13

EMBER

The knock comes as promptly as usual, but it's missing its demanding rap. "I'm not feeling well today," I call from the other side of the door, clutching my cardigan over my chest and not bothering to even crack the door.

"Do you need anything?" Grimm asks.

"No, I'm okay."

The floorboards don't creak. I sense he's still pressed against the door, hoping for more. Finally, he sighs. "I'll be back later today to see if you need anything. I'm leaving the keys to the truck on the rocking chair out here. Feel free to drive into town if you're up for it."

I don't know what I expected after yesterday, but it isn't this. Perhaps I don't give Grimm enough credit. He has shown me a mix of personality types, yet I always end up out of harm's way, my needs being met.

Sleep came to me easily the night before. My mind whirled with thoughts—what I had witnessed, what I had revealed, my ingrained beliefs, Grimm's lips against mine—but the tears flowing from my eyes knocked me out. I awoke even more confused than the day before and with no more tears to lull me back to slumber. One thing is for certain: I can't be near Grimm, at least not right now. I need more time to clear my head and focus.

Grimm breathes heavily from the other side of the door before walking down the steps and crunching over the grass to the opening of the woods. I suppose a normal woman wouldn't be able to tell these things just from their hearing alone, but that's the problem. I'm not normal. I've known it my whole life. It's just another reason why I must stay vigilant to protect myself and others.

Once I'm certain Grimm is far enough away, I exit the cottage, scanning the area just to be sure. I push myself through the line of trees. I've always been stealthy, my footsteps light. I may not entirely be a Were—thank God. The only physical evidence is my tail, my ears, and my glowing eyes, but my senses and movements resemble those of a fox.

I find time whenever I can to explore the woods around me. I can sense them, another ability I discovered since arriving in Dayton, which makes this all so much easier. It's been hard to find time away from Grimm's view. He usually tries to avoid me, yet he's always nearby. Faking illness won't raise suspicion, but my mission still exists, and makes this excuse of absence from my job even more rewarding.

I follow their scent, stronger as I reach deeper into the woods. As I approach the clearing, their laughter greets my transformed, furry ears. I peek through the brush guarding me, squatting down so I'm hidden. I pull out my phone, angling the camera at a blank spot in the greenery and zooming in on the center of the open space. It's a group of children, running in circles, unattended by guardians. Shame washes over me. Of course, werewolves start as children, just like I did. It's not their fault that their parents nurtured their true selves, stayed in communities with others like them, and let them grow into their abilities. It feels wrong to film and exploit them.

My father had other Hunters film me during testing when I was a young child. I hated it, but it's hard to say if it was because my shame was recorded for others to study, or because the prodding, seclusion, and rejection of needs for me to reach my breaking point and shift on command. Probably a mixture of all the above. Luckily for me, the testing didn't last long. My father only let it happen for a few years once my ears and tails presented themself. He didn't want me growing used to transforming. He wanted it to stop. I wasn't bred to be a fighter like other Hunters. I was an heir, supposed to carry on his family lineage, not used as a weapon. He had no idea where my perversions came from. Neither he nor my late mother were part Were. He assumed my mother must have cheated on him, or that there were Were genes somewhere down my family line. He had no one to take out his anger on for my genetic disabilities except me, since my mother died in childbirth. I accepted the rage, the disgust. It wasn't anything different than how I felt.

I wanted to prove myself and do something useful, so I left—and so far, I'd done a good job. I never intended to be Grimm's prisoner, and although I hate the man, especially the confusing way he makes me feel, it turned out to be the perfect situation to aid my cause. My phone storage is full of content to reveal the Weres for the monsters they truly are. Except now, as I ready my thumb to press record, everything I grew up learning about these beasts seems blurry—harder to focus on.

I drop my phone, watching as a little boy shifts partially into a wolf form, ears and a tail much like my own, except not belonging to a fox. The other young girl and boy laugh as he strains, holding his fingers in front of his face, I assume to reveal his claws. Instead of the points emerging from his fingertips, he farts. The three roar with laughter. A small chuckle escapes my lips, and I palm my mouth to stop more.

I can't do it. I can't record these three children so full of joy, so unaware of people like me ready to shred the fibers of their security blanket. This realization is more than just the silliness of their farts or how cute they look as they pretend to fight each other—so much has changed since I escaped my childhood home, not just from what I've witnessed but from what I've felt. I shifted in front of Grimm, and he wasn't repulsed. Of course, it seems obvious, since he's a Were too, but the look in his eyes, the passion behind his lips—it's almost like revealing my truth made me more worth wanting instead of the opposite.

Throughout my life, I have learned that the hidden part of myself was a mistake against nature. I can't control how I was born, but I could choose how I behaved. Not everyone was meant for the outside world or for a full life. I could isolate. I could utilize the skills I've learned throughout my life to bring good to the world by being invisible. Yet, if that part of me was so inherently evil, why did it feel so good to break free, to be seen and wanted? Perhaps it's my lady-bits talking. I wanted Grimm everywhere. I wanted him to touch me in places I only let my fingers explore in secret. Despite my isolation, I'd been exposed to the world through the media. I'm aware of our power dynamic and the role Grimm plays to someone like me, someone who's lived a life alone. His attention may feel special, but in reality, it could just be a means to distract me.

I can't decide. Everything is too much, too fast. One thing is sure: what I'm doing right now, or trying to do, is wrong. I feel it in the depths of my marrow. These children are innocent and don't need to be exploited. I shove my phone away, crawling out from my hiding place and slinking through the woods in which I came.

It's a good thing I faked being sick today. I need time alone. Except my whole life has been me alone. Perhaps I need company—with someone who I can't seem to get out of my head.

14

GRIMM

Despite my need to stay focused at the office today, I couldn't. The situation has gotten out of hand. After a prompt call to the DOS, they assured me they'd be sending more support to combat the amateur Hunters flooding the area. I should be prepping for their arrival, creating strategies with the leaders in my pack to keep my people safe. I found some time to do what's necessary, but there's always more I could be doing. Instead, all I can think about is her. Is she really sick, or is she just so distraught after everything that happened yesterday? From surviving a life-or-death situation, to revealing her true form, to sharing a moment with me that never should have happened—I can only imagine the inner turmoil she's going through.

It's not even the end of the day yet. The clock above my office door reads 3:30, but I must get home and make sure she's okay. I've told her she's not my prisoner, but I need to spell it out for her. She's free to go whenever she wants. I'd even give her enough money to get her on her feet. It's the least I can do after tasting her and pulling her body against mine. The thought of her leaving creates a hollow void in my stomach, but it's not about me. She doesn't deserve to feel trapped. She's clearly lived her life hating herself. I wish I could show her just how special she is, but that's a job for someone else, someone who doesn't want to run their tongue along her seam and make her cry from pleasure. It must be someone who has nothing to gain from her. My dick would surely benefit if I allowed myself to take her. It would be selfish and inappropriate, especially in her current state.

But I can't just tell her to go. I need to explain myself, to make her see that she's beautiful and I'm not repulsed by her true form. She has a home with me, but it's not her only option. She deserves better than an old creep like me.

I get up from my office chair, my plan already coming into view. I'll make her dinner, invite her over, and clear the air. I race home, contemplating shifting to speed up the journey, but decide otherwise. It's not worth ruining a nice set of clothes to get home a few minutes quicker.

Ember's cottage comes into view. I hold my breath as I study the small house, worried she took my keys and left for good. I wouldn't blame her, but I don't want her to leave in a state of fear, without enough to make herself comfortable. I breathe out once I see the light to the living room turn on and her silhouetted form behind the sheer kitchen curtains.

I hurry the rest of the way home, then pull out meat, pasta, tomatoes, and onions. This will be the first meal I make for her. I wish it could be something more impressive than spaghetti and meat sauce, but it's the quickest meal to prepare, and I don't want to waste any more time inside my head.

After an hour, I turn the skillet down to low heat to let the sauce simmer, then change into a pair of gray linen pants and a white t-shirt. I fix my hair obsessively, douse myself in cologne, examine my pores, and fuss with my nose hairs. It's stupid. This isn't about looking good for her. This is potentially our last meal together, but I can't help but hope for more, because I'm a sick, weak male, of course.

Finally, after every inch of myself is inspected and groomed, I exit my house and make the short walk to Ember's cottage. It's still daylight. She'll probably think I'm even more of a grandpa for suggesting dinner so early, but I let that worry ruminate in my mind, choosing not to act on it.

Every morning, I stand on her front porch and knock, ready to guide her to work, but it's different now. It's as nerve-wracking as it was this morning, yet now my intentions for being here are more implicit. After what feels like a lifetime of uncertainty, I knock.

Surprisingly, Ember opens it quickly, as if she were waiting for me, but that would be crazy. She's freshly showered, her hair combed back and flat against her scalp. She wears a simple white slip set, no bra. If I'd only been a little bit quicker in making the journey here, I could have caught her in a state of undress. Perhaps clutching a towel to her chest. I shake away the thought, clearing my throat and shifting on my feet. "Hi. I wanted to see if you'd want to have dinner at my place. That is if you're feeling up to it."

Her eyes grow slightly, and she turns to look behind her. A jealous thought pops into my head, imagining another man in the room with her. Of course, that's crazy. I don't deserve to be jealous. She opens the door wider, studying me, and I can't help but notice her pupils dilate. "Okay, sure."

I hardly believe it's that easy. She always puts up a fight, and after running away from me last night and avoiding me this morning, I thought I'd have to do a lot more pleading. I can't help the stupid smile creeping up my cheeks. "Great." I tuck my hands in my pockets. "I hope you like spaghetti and meat sauce."

She steps out onto the porch with me, crossing her arms over her pebbled breasts. "It beats the can of soup I was about to pry open and shove into the microwave."

"You mean, after putting it into a bowl first, right? The microwave would catch on fire if you just put the can in."

She sighs, walking past me and going down the steps. "I guess it's a good thing you came when you did, then, or who knows what I would owe you after I burned down your guest house."

My heart stops, and my throat tightens. I'm supposed to be making her feel better, not aggravating her further. I'm about to apologize when she turns around, walking backward, and smirks at me. I think it's the first time I've ever seen a smile sent my way from her. It's hypnotizing, and I nearly teeter off the steps from how lost I am in it. She carries on to my house, not checking to see if I'm following. I suppress my giddiness, pushing down my hope of the evening, even as my stupid cock bulges against the seam of my pants. I should have worn something heavier than linen. Perhaps metal underwear.

I jog after her, keeping a small distance until we get to my back porch, and I run ahead to open the kitchen door for her. She gives me a nod before stepping inside. "Wow," she says after taking a swiveling look around my kitchen—an open concept leading into the living room and dining room. "You really are rich."

I cough. "Oh, um, I wouldn't say that."

"What would you say then?" She walks backward, trailing her finger over my black and white marble counter.

I follow after her, hands behind my back. "I'm older, established."

"You're not that old."

"How old do you think I am?"

She taps her lip, eyes searching. I want to stay under her scrutiny for an eternity. "Thirty-five."

I laugh. "Funny."

"Older?"

"Forty-three."

She shrugs, our chests nearly touching now. She dodges out of my way and takes a seat on the stool facing the kitchen island. "That's not that old."

I go to the stove and pull out two bowls. "Not that old for what?" I glance at her as I serve us both a helping of spaghetti.

She shrugs, her cheeks pink. She doesn't respond, the air around us heavy with the suggestion.

I clear my throat. "Would you like some wine?"

"Sure!" she says, jostling out of her stupor.

I grab a red from the rack next to the stove, not mentioning that it's the most expensive one of the bunch. I pour her a glass and hand it to her. I pour myself one, losing focus as she makes a gagging sound. "You don't like it?"

"Is wine supposed to taste rotten?"

I take a sip, swirling the velvety liquid around my mouth. It's fucking great shit. Realization dawns on me. "Is this your first time drinking wine?"

She shakes her head, takes a gulp as her face morphs in disgust. "Yes, I'm only twenty."

My cock loses the semi I've been sporting all evening. Sometimes I swear I feel the same on the inside as I did when I was twenty years old, but the reminder of just how young she is makes me want to vomit.

She must notice how uncomfortable her words make me because she laughs. "Did you forget?"

"Yes, twenty is just very young."

"Very young for what?" She raises an eyebrow at me, downing the rest of the wine and pushing her empty glasses back to me.

I chuckle at her implication, my cock back to being harder than ever. I shake my head. "No more."

"Why?" she whines.

"Let's eat first. You drank that way too fast, and if you've never drunk before, it's going to hit you hard without food in your stomach." I strategically grab the two bowls and my still-full glass of wine, leading her to the dining room table, in view from the kitchen.

She giggles, grabbing her empty glass and the bottle before following after me. "I think I already feel it."

I shake my head, quickly place the food down before running to pull her chair out, and pluck the bottle from her hand. "Then I have some catching up to do." I take a swig and walk to my seat at the other end of the table.

"Hey!" She whines with a red-stained smile, still gorgeous.

"Eat up."

She groans but swirls her fork in the pasta, taking a large bite. "This is good!" She says with her mouth full, her cheeks all rosy. It's a horrible thought, but I'm glad she's so quickly buzzed from the wine. It's giving me a chance to see her true self, her carefree self, without her usual high walls. I smile as I take my own bite, the happiness warming my edges, but I don't let it get too far, suddenly remembering the point of this whole dinner.

I clear my throat and straighten my shoulders. "The reason I asked you to dinner is to apologize."

"For what?" she asks, her mouth full. I'm usually a stickler about table manners, but everything she does is adorable. I can't let her behavior cloud my train of thought.

"For yesterday, in my truck."

Her eyes widen, and the sparkle in her pupils dims. She focuses on her food, silent.

"I shouldn't have kissed you," I say. "That was inappropriate."

"Right." She nods, still not meeting my eyes.

"I want you to know, you don't have to stay here. You're right. I have enough money. I don't need you to pay me back for the car. I don't know what has gotten into me lately. I think it's just the stress from the Hunters and everything going on in the media. I took it out on you, and you don't deserve that. I'll even give you enough so you can get settled."

"Are you firing me?" she asks, wounded.

"No. Of course, not. If you want to stay, you're welcome to. I just can't imagine why you'd want that."

I ready for her retort, for her to agree before accepting her freedom, but only silence follows. She continues eating, more focused now and less carefree. She's torturing me. Of course, I have feelings for her. Just yesterday, her lips pressed against mine, and I clung to her like a lifeline. But I didn't anticipate I'd want her to stay so badly. I can't stomach another bite, hanging on her response.

She finishes her food and nudges the plate forward, bringing a white napkin to wipe her lips. "I think I'll stay."

"You will?" I say the words too fast, too excited.

She nods—gone is the tipsy young woman, and in her place sits someone entirely sure of herself. "I think I have more to learn about your world, about myself."

I smile. "I agree."

She shrugs. "Besides, you can't beat the view." She turns, glancing at the lake behind her, and the setting sun dances across its surface.

I don't take my eyes off her. "You definitely can't."

She turns back to me, a contented look across her face. A long table separates us, and yet I've never felt closer to her under her gaze—not her hatred, or fear, or loathing, something polar opposite but just as strong. The sticky silence becomes too much, and I decide to break it before it swallows me whole. "More wine?"

"Sure."

I walk to the other side, pour a glass while keeping my distance to not ruin the moment too soon. She takes a large sip, and by the time I'm back to my seat, it's nearly halfway gone. "Ember, you don't drink wine like that."

"Why?" she asks with a grimace. "It's gross, I want to get it over with."

"It's a 200-dollar bottle of wine; it's meant to be savored."

"Damn. You're good at wasting money." She downs the other half and smiles.

"Maybe so." I chug my own glass, not wanting to leave the sober dynamics unchecked. Suddenly, our food is gone, and it's not a good idea to drink any more. The sun dips below the northern windows, casting a warm glow that illuminates the house in a cozy yet haunting light.

"Got any games?" Ember asks. The question shocks me. She has no intention of leaving.

I stutter a response. "Monopoly?"

"No Twister?"

I'm like a prepubescent teenager, my heart pattering in my chest at her cheeky smile. She's aware of her effect, and she's toying with me. This alone is the most exciting game I'll ever experience.

"Maybe next time." I stand, and she follows me into the living room, where I pull out a board game from a shelf.

It takes a while for the wine to wear off. I barely notice it, the night is still light and giddy even after several hours sitting around my coffee table. There's never really an end to Monopoly, at least not one I've ever experienced, but we're both real estate moguls, arguing over a board completely covered in plastic buildings.

"Why won't you sell me the boardwalk? I have all the other blues. What are you going to do with it?"

"Keep it from you."

She laughs, falling to her back. "Why?" she asks the ceiling.

"'Cause it's funny."

"I hate this game." I can't see her smile, but I hear it.

"What board game do you prefer?"

"I don't know. This is the first one I've ever played."

"You've never played a board game?" It was obvious to me that she never played Monopoly when I had to go over the instructions in heavy detail, but I'd never guessed she hadn't played *any* board games at all. We did grow up in a different time, but surely it couldn't be *that* different.

She sits up, her humor lost, and she tucks a strand of hair behind her ear. "I mean, I've seen people play them on TV."

For most of the night, I forgot about her innocence, but now, as she sits before me, her eyes looking anywhere but mine, her knees tucked into herself, I'm reminded of all the little, strange comments. It hurts me. Yes, she's young, but she should have had more experiences. She seems to be lacking an entire lifetime. I want to question, but she's just starting to trust me. I don't want to scare her away right when I'm finally in her good graces.

"Well, it seems we have a lot to catch up on."

She smiles, her previous shame gone. "What should we play next?"

I shrug. "I heard Twister is pretty fun."

She laughs, falling back and hitting her head on the corner of the armchair on her way down. "Ow."

I crawl over to her, smiling as I stare down at her, rubbing at the assaulted spot. "Are you okay?" I ask.

"I think I have a concussion."

"Oh yeah?" I run my fingers through her hair, and she drops her hand. I replace the pressure on the spot, searching for a knot. "I think you'll survive." Our gaze intertwines as I hold my body over hers.

She wets her lips. "I don't know. I might have to call out of work tomorrow."

I shake my head. "You can do whatever you want, Ember."

"Anything?" She arches subtly.

"I'm putty in your hands."

Her eyes flutter close, and her lips part. I lean down, our mouths meeting. She moans as she opens for me and her hands find the back of my neck and explore my scalp.

I press into her, gently at first, testing the waters, but her lower half grinds into my hardened length. I'm thankful for the linen pants now, wishing I were wearing less. The alcohol is out of my system, and surely out of Ember's, too, as it's been several hours, but I'm not thinking clearly. I need every inch of her, to taste, to smell, to fuck. I kiss her, and she returns my passion. My hands trail down her side, playing at the hem of her shirt. I'm prepared to take my time, to make sure this is something she absolutely wants, but she reaches in between us and pulls her top over her head, breaking away from my lips to remove it from her body.

"Fuck," I groan into her mouth as I palm her bare breasts, pebbled under my touch.

"Oh, God," she whimpers as she spreads, and I seat myself between her legs. Her skirt rides up, and only her cotton panties separate me from her cunt. Is she wet for me already? She sounds like it, smells like it. I must feel for myself. One hand remains at her breasts while my other travels down the side of her, trailing up her leg as she raises them to cage me in.

I tease her with my touches, getting closer but then pulling away. "Please," she begs into my mouth. It's exactly the words I need to hear.

I don't have time to pull her panties down. I push them to the side, moving over to reach her and grinding against her leg as I tease at her seam. I bury my head in the crook of her neck, needing her lips off mine just to ground myself. "God, Ember. You're so wet." My fingers dance in her moisture. "Grimm," she whimpers. She wants more, and I'm prepared to give her everything, every inch of me, but the begging is too sweet, and I want this to last.

I spread her lips apart, sweeping through her valleys. She's so soft. Instead of my fingers, I imagine my cock, piercing through her, getting my dick slippery so I can slip in easily. I find her hole, pressing into her. She cries out. "God, you're tight, Ember. You're going to need me to fuck you with my finger for hours just so I can get halfway inside." I mean it. I might come in my pants soon, but I can harden up again by the time I'm done stretching her out.

I take a break, swiping up to find the sensitive bud at the top of her cunt. "Jesus Christ!" she yells. I've barely even applied pressure. Her body is like a puzzle I want to take apart and put back together. There are a thousand combinations of ways I can make her come, but I can tell from the quickening of her breath and her nails digging into my back, even though my shirt, that she's so close.

I'm too tempted. I prop myself up on my elbow so I can watch her as I return my attention to her clit. She's angelic, a goddess. I must witness her come. I circle her, slowly at first but gently increasing my speed and pressure. Her cries build. There's never been sweeter music in my home. She's bringing every corner to life. I don't even notice that I'm growing more frantic against her legs, that the building pressure at the base of my spine isn't just from watching her near the brink of breaking, but from grinding against her.

She screams—loud, glorious, her breast vibrating in my palm as the pleasure washes over her. It's too much, and before I even register it, I've reached my edge too, coming into my pants. I don't have time to be mortified at myself. I'm too busy soaking in every inch of her, her body still twitching as she floats down from her orgasm.

Fluffy ears burst up at the crown of her head, and as she blinks her eyes open, they change from green to golden. She must notice, either from feeling it herself or watching my eyes track the change. She reaches up, covering the furry peaks with her hands. "No, oh my God. No."

I place my hand over hers. "Shhh. No. You're beautiful, Ember."

She wiggles from under me, pushing me away, and I sit up, too worried about her to be concerned about the wet spot at the front of my pants. Tears form in her eyes, and I can't help but notice the tail sweeping the floor from the bottom of her skirt. "No. It's getting worse. I'm losing control. I need to go." She stands, and I follow after her, reaching for her as she adjusts her clothing. "Sometimes it's good to lose control," I say. It's a crazy statement coming from me—the person who thrives on order, but maybe with her, I'm willing to become someone different.

"No, you don't understand." She pulls away, rushing away from me.

The shame comes tenfold. I'm much too aware of the cum lining my pants, so much so that it's dripping down my shin. It's my age. It's the whole situation. This was a mistake. How could I let myself get so clouded?

Before she's gone into the night, she stops at the door, her eyes meeting mine. "I'm sorry. I'm just dealing with myself."

I rush toward her, but she backs away. "It's okay. Maybe this was too fast. I will help you learn how to control your powers. I promise."

She nods. "Thank you." She turns to her cabin, running away into the night, running away from me. Again.

15

EMBER

It turns out my job isn't so boring now that I have actual work to do. I welcome the distraction, thankful for a busy mind and hands so I don't have to reflect on everything that happened last night, or the past few days in general.

Grimm picked me up this morning as usual, not as early, and also with a cup of coffee in one hand and a bacon, egg, and cheese sandwich in the other. He smiled at me, timid and searching, but a smile nonetheless. Maybe I should let him fuck me with his hand more often. Joking. Because even though I've *never* experienced something as wonderful as I did last night, it was a mistake. There are so many reasons. The main one is because of who I am. Throw in the age gap, the unequal power dynamic, and the itching I feel whenever I'm in his presence as if I must stuff my hands away so as not to grab him—it's a recipe for disaster.

I left his house crying, running to my cottage—again. Something's wrong with me, but everything is just too much. My feelings for him don't make sense, and my inability to control myself concerns me. I believe him when he tells me I'm beautiful, that the deformed version of myself doesn't repulse him, but it doesn't make me any less vulnerable. I'm programmed to hate myself. Words from a sweet man won't replace the years of shame I grew up around.

I've been waiting for this moment. Grimm's giving me access to everything. He brought over file after file into my office. Each one describes the members of his community. He filled me in on the details. As I already knew, they're not a wildlife conservation organization protecting against poachers. He's the Minister of a secret society of werewolves. Obviously, their existence isn't surprising to me, considering what I am. Besides, the entire world seems to be aware of werewolves now, and according to social media, almost everyone has accepted their existence. Whether or not they need to be destroyed, well, that's still up for debate.

Grimm asked me to review the list of members and ensure everyone was safe and not alone. He wanted me to spread the news about what happened the other day because he feared calling a council meeting would be too dangerous. It was the first time he spoke to me while looking me in the eye. He's nervous around me now, I can tell. It's not his fault. I'm confusing, even to myself. I've taken a picture of every member's file with my phone. Weeks ago, sending this information would have been easy for me. I hated myself and hated everyone who shared my sickness and chose to live with it and repopulate. Now everything's different.

I finally notice the time at the top of my screen. It's pushing 7 pm. It's easy to lose track of time since my office has no windows, and I've been busy the entire day. My stomach rumbles. I haven't even had time for lunch. I should check on Grimm, see if he needs anything else, and suggest we leave for the day, but instead, I scroll through my phone, going through all the content I've accumulated since arriving in Dayton. Past me would be proud. Current me hates myself.

I continue to scroll. There aren't many photos, as most of my life has been spent indoors, surrounded by only my family and people who worked for us. I finally get to the top of the camera roll. It's a video I took of the computer screen in my father's office. It's me when I was a child, with even brighter hair tied up in pigtails and green eyes two times too large for my face. I'm strapped to a metal table in a sterile medical lab. A scientist in a white lab coat brings a tool to my arm. It's funny, when I saw this video many years ago, I had forgotten the instrument. I suppose my mind had hidden the memory, but seeing it replayed before me brought everything back. It was kind of like an ear-piercing gun, not as strong, but it poked my arm with a needle. Not enough to draw blood, but enough to hurt. Little me screams with each press of the button on the back of the tool. I rub at my arm, the memories of the sting coming in full force. No one comes for me. No one comforts me. The scientist continues to inflict pain until I shift. Claws emerge from my fingertips, my back arches as my tail bursts from underneath me. My ears pop just above my pink hair ties.

Finally, he stops. More men come in. One of them is my father. They examine me and measure my deformities while I cry endlessly. I barely notice the tears now flowing from my eyes until I turn off my phone and wipe them off my cheek. It's been years since something like that has happened to me. My father promised—and kept it—that if I let the scientists run their test to figure out the extent of my illness, I'd never have to endure it again. I'd spend the rest of my life in the comfort of home, alone, learning to keep my abilities hidden. At the time, when he knelt before me, holding my little hands, it felt like a gift, but as I grew older, the isolation swallowed me whole. I would rather endure the pain just to be with people again—real people, not just my nanny, my tutor, the actors on TV, or the people I witnessed on the other side of social media.

I shake my sorrow away, the tears running down my face becoming too much, and pick up my phone to search for the number of the local Chinese restaurant. Grimm is usually the one to tell me it's time to go home, promptly at 5 pm, but it doesn't seem like he's coming soon. Whether he's too nervous to be in my presence or drowning in work, it's evident that I need to take the lead and get us something to eat. It's the least I can do. He did feed me and send me to another dimension last night after all.

I place a large order to be delivered to my cottage. Grimm would lose his shit if I had them deliver the food here. I sneak out, pressing my ear to Grimm's office door to make sure he's still in before leaving. Sure enough, I make out his gruff voice, muttering under his breath as he clicks away.

It only takes me fifteen minutes to retrieve the food and return to the stone office. I'm thankful I started getting the hang of the location and even paid attention to the secret knock that let me in. I must ask Grimm whether or not that's a technological security feature, or some sort of werewolf magic.

I tiptoe to Grimm's office, tapping on the door. "Come in!" he yells. When I push my way inside, his eyes remain on his screen as he continues to press on his keys ravenously. Behind him, his projected window illuminates the room with an artificial silver moon. "What is it?"

"I brought takeout." I hold up the large paper bag.

His eyes pop to mine, and he straightens before jumping out of his seat to rush to me. "Oh God, Ember. I'm so sorry."

My cheeks heat, his gaze on me is too much. His silver-streaked hair glows in the fake moonlight, his features sharper from the shadows. It's good we spent the majority of the day away from each other, even if only a thin wall separated us. My hunger for food leaves, and in its place throbs something harder to ignore. "It's okay." I walk in, place the bag on his circular table in the corner, and pull out its contents.

He glances at his watch. "Shit. It's late. You don't have to stay here. I still have some things to wrap up, but you can take the food to go." I'd think he wants me to leave if not for the look in his eyes as he steps closer to me, timid as if I'll skitter away with any sudden movement.

I take a seat, opening a box of lo mein and letting the heat hit my face to resurface my reasoning. "I'll eat here. You should take a break, and then I can help you with anything else when we're finished."

He pulls out a seat, sighing. "You don't have to do that."

I chuckle. "I'm your assistant after all. It's my job to assist you."

He opens a set of chopsticks and digs into the carton of sweet-and-sour chicken. "Yes, you're my assistant, not my slave. You don't have to work after business hours because I'm anal-retentive."

"Grimm, I haven't been doing much the last few weeks. It's the least I can do."

"That's not your fault,"" he says between bites. "I'm the one who wouldn't fill you in on the actual job."

I shrug, but it's true. It's crazy that our conversation feels so normal, like a regular boss-employee exchange. It's only been a day since he slid his fingers inside me and caressed me until I cried out, and not even a week since I wanted to wring his neck. Kiss him, yes, but still wring his neck.

My hunger may have been replaced in his presence, but my body needed this meal. It only takes about fifteen minutes for both of us to scarf down several cartons of noodles, rice, and sauce-covered meat.

"How did it go with the phone calls? Did anyone give you a hard time?" he asks, leaning back in his chair.

I shake my head. "A few people seemed concerned about who I was, but after I explained I was your assistant, they all gave this little knowing *ohhh*."

"Knowing *ohhh?*"

"Yeah, like they've heard about me."

He rolls his eyes and crosses his arms over his chest. His biceps appear as if they're about to burst free, the veins in his hands prominent. God, it must be painful to be so well-built.

"I told the pack I had an assistant. Were they welcoming at least?"

"I mean, I was telling them that they might be in danger and not to be alone. They didn't necessarily want to get to know me after that."

He tenses. "Right. I'm sorry." He keeps apologizing. It would be annoying if he weren't so adorable. "We'll have a council meeting next week, and you can come along. I think it would be good to meet others like you." He stirs around his unfinished fried rice.

A deep-seated part of me cringes at his words—others like me. I never viewed my differences as abilities, only flaws, but the new, more conscious part of myself knows he's right. "Yeah, that would be good. I was thinking about reaching out to Red, you know, since she offered." I look at my own spicy broccoli, no longer hungry, but feeling uncomfortable with exposing just how desperate I am for connection.

"Oh yeah, definitely!" He pulls out his phone, swipes through, and slides it across the table, Red's number displayed on the screen.

"I just realized we don't have each other's numbers." I blush. I've never been so intimate with another person and yet, there's still so much we don't know about each other—more him than me.

He pulls his phone back when I push it toward him after depositing Red's info into my own phone. "Well, it helps that we're neighbors. If I need you, I can just knock on your door."

"True."

"I think it's good you want to meet with her." He leans forward, his hand just inches from mine. "I want you to feel at home here."

I laugh without humor, falling back into my seat. "Well, I ran away from home, so I don't think you want it to feel like that."

His expression grows serious. "Do you want to talk about it?"

I look away, crossing my arms over my chest. "No." Why do I insist on acting like a child? Half of it is deep-buried pain, half of it is the fact that he'd probably kill me—literally—if he found out the truth.

He sighs. "Well, I'll tell you this, from what I gathered, it sounds like where you came from wasn't a place full of love. Instead of teaching you how special you are, they made you feel less than. You're beautiful and wonderful, in every form."

Tears form from a hidden well. I clench my fists with my arms crossed, attempting to fight my emotions. "You don't know me in every form."

He gets up, moving to a chair closer to me, leaning over to cup my jaw. "True, but from what I've seen, I can't imagine viewing you any less lovely. In fact, please show me something ugly, because I can't take the blinding brightness anymore."

His words should fix something inside of me—perhaps they do, but only anger surfaces. He doesn't know the truth, and if he did, all his sweet words would turn sour. No matter what side I'm on, I'm always disgusting. I break free from his grasp, standing and turning toward the door, tears streaming down my face. He's so quick. I barely take a step before he's in front of me, looming down, his eyes focused and his lips set into a hard line. He grabs my arm, backing me against a wall.

"What are you doing?" I ask, trying to pry off his hand, despite the tingling under my skin.

He presses in more. "Tell me to stop complimenting you. Tell me to keep my distance. Tell me what to do."

"You're a grown man. I don't need to tell you what to do."

He growls, low in his throat. It's almost so subtle that I miss it. My body sure doesn't. Even as I fight his restraint on me, the lower half of me grinds into him. "What do you want, Ember?" He mumbles, his neck arching slightly.

I don't know what's happening. Moments ago, I was hurting, and I wanted away from this man who opened the rough shell surrounding my heart. Now goosebumps line my skin, and my thin dress and his dark slacks and button-down feel like the heaviest garments in the world. I want him closer, all over me, to kiss away the pain, to touch every inch in hopes that I'll feel the warmth I've always so desperately craved. I can't tell him this, though. Yes, as he looks at me, his chest expanding in heavy breaths, it seems as if he might feel the same, but what I feel is too much. There's no way to admit the truth of my longing and come out unscathed. It would hurt both of us whenever reality reveals itself.

Instead, I opt for a simpler response, one that doesn't sound as desperate. "Kiss me." The words barely leave my lips before he crashes against me. One hand grabs the base of my neck, the other wraps around my waist, raising me up and pulling me in. My feet graze the ground, the sensation of nails and fur at my throat. He's shifting against me, his body expanding, his shirt pulling taut. I'm unsure if it's a mimicking behavior, but I shift as well. Pressure builds at my crown and behind me.

I push back, actually able to move him this time. I want more of him, but I'm too repulsed. His kind words and tender touches can't erase the years of self-loathing.

He studies me, concerned at first, but when he notices my ears at the top of my head, his expression changes. I take a step to flee, but he grabs me by my wrist. Despite my newfound strength, I'm unable to break free from his grasp. "Is this it? Is this your full form?"

"What do you mean?"

"Is it just the ears, the tail, and the eyes, or are you holding back?"

"No, it's never been more than this." I don't tell him the truth—that I'm using everything in me to keep this form hidden. Who knows what would pop free if I truly let my guard down?

He chuckles, and the sound quickly burns my cheeks, making me want to cause violence.

"Do you want to see what a real monster looks like?" He steps back, revealing more of himself in the projected moonlight.

I don't answer, watching as he shifts before my eyes, his clothes falling in pieces to the ground. Black, silky fur covers his form—except it's not his form anymore. Standing on four paws is a wolf, massive, with silver eyes, piercing through the night. I've been trained my whole life to fear and despise these creatures, but I'm overwhelmed by his beauty, his power, his grace as he stalks closer to me.

He licks his chops as he sizes me up. He presses me back up against the wall, his fangs at my ear. I'm ready for him to devour me, lost in a trance only explained by mysticism. "Do I disgust you?" He steps back, no longer in his wolf form, but not human either. His body is still large, covered in black hair, but he stands on two feet. His face is his own, but also different, more intense, with two elongated ears and hair trailing over his jaw. I follow the hard muscle of his bare chest, down his defined abdomen, even lower. I gasp.

He steps close enough for me to reach down and touch him. I can't look away. I'm salivating. I've never seen a man so exposed in real life, but I've had access to the internet. It isn't normal—inhumanly large, slick, the tip smaller at the top, and dripping with lubrication. A deflated bulge sits at the base, right above a tight sack.

My fingers twitch, but before I can grab him, he steps back, lathering his clawed hand with his slick release and tugging down his length. "I could come just from looking at you like this, frightened, mesmerized, perfect."

I'm still in my Were form. He's touching himself, holding back moans as he gazes upon me, my hidden self revealed. The truth of his attraction is evident. There's no talking myself out of it. Something like power surges through me. I've always been ashamed, but in this lust-filled haze, I can't find that familiar feeling. I want him to watch me, and I'm afraid his attention will end. I reach for the straps of my thin dress, letting the fabric fall off my shoulder. My eyes stay locked to his as I pull down my bra straps and shimmy out of my lace underwear.

He slows, turning his head. "Fuck, Ember."

I've never been so exposed. I'm complete myself, even if there's a small part of me still holding back.

"Do you know how to touch yourself?" he asks. Is my innocence so apparent? Sure, I've felt the urge on particularly lonesome nights, but they were few and unsatisfying. My words are almost too heavy to leave me; his taunting is an excruciating form of foreplay. "Not like you."

"I can show you. I can teach you so many things, but I just want to watch you like this. You're so beautiful, bare for me, letting your true self through."

I enjoy his attention. I never thought that would be the case, but God, it's torturous. "Please, touch me." My knees buckle, and I must lean against the stone wall to keep from falling, but Grimm swoops in, holding me in his arms. "Just because you asked so sweetly." He kisses my lips, his hands running down my body until he reaches my breast, palming the weight.

He shudders, moans spilling into my mouth. "Do you like this?" he asked, toying with my nipple.

"Yes." He could touch any part of me and I'd melt further, but this seems too much.

My breathing increases as his fingers dance more rapidly. "Look at you, you're about to come just from this. Do you even realize that?"

"Please." I don't know what I'm begging for, but something feels close and urgent. I groan as his hand leaves my nipple, traveling across my middle until he meets my pounding heat. He grazes my seam, and my world spins as I scream.

"Shh."

This isn't the first time he's touched me like this, only a day before, but the anticipation, the war of emotions, all of it has built up into something I'm not sure I'll survive.

He applies more pressure, parting me. "God, you're so wet." I need more, but he pulls away, dropping to his knees. He looks up at me, eyes wide and glassy, the only soft thing about him in his form of fur and fangs. "Can I taste you?"

I don't even think. "Yes," I say around a sob. Nothing sounds sweeter. His fingers trail up my body, cupping my ass and bringing me closer to him. He moves me up slightly, holding me in his hands and pressing me more against the wall. Both monstrous hands cup my ass, and his finger circles the base of my tail. "Oh my God!" I've never felt anything so wonderful, never had someone touch that part of me. His hot breath flutters across my skin, and I cry out louder.

"Your sounds, your scent. I can't take it anymore." His long tongue parts me, lapping through me. "Oh, God." His words don't stop his eagerness. A small part of me worries about the fangs, but he either snapped them back or has so much skill that I don't feel any ounce of pain—only pleasure, a blinding, overwhelming wave of pleasure.

His attention moves to the spot at the top. Circling moves with rigid pressure. "Fuck!" I cry. Who knew something could feel so glorious? It's just like the pressure from his fingers, but slicker, more intense, and more intimate. I glance down, catching him watching me as he devours me, his mouth glistening under the moonlight, his eyes wild. Just the sight adds another layer. Something snaps within me, like a glow stick releasing a burst of euphoria. I'm lost, screaming, and convulsing. The sensation is too much, and my body fights against it subconsciously, but he holds me in place, thankfully, because I can't get enough. He doesn't stop until the wave pulls back to sea, and my nerves settle.

He kisses up my body, soft, but his fangs graze against my skin as if he can't hold back much longer. He laps my neck up to my ear, causing me to shiver when he whispers, "What do you want?"

"More. I want you inside of me." This is my first time. Everything with him is my first. He knows I'm innocent, but I'm unsure if he knows I'm a virgin.

"Are you sure?" he asks, one hand running circles around my nipple and the other reaching between my legs.

"Yes." I am sure. I've never been more sure of anything in my life. I can't explain my feelings for this man, but he makes me feel so good, so unlike myself, and I *need* more.

He dips inside me, and I shudder. "Still so wet for me." He inserts another finger. "I'm going to stretch you out."

"Please."

He flips my body around, and I brace myself against the wall, breath heavy from the sudden force. My tail rests against my bare back between us. For the first time, I don't feel the urge to push it away. I want it splayed against me as he fucks me.

He keeps his fingers inside of me, pumping in and out, adding another one. The pressure builds. He leans over me, making me feel small under him. "I don't have a condom. Maybe I should just fuck you like this until you come all over my hand."

Although I'm sure he'd make it wonderful, the thought of him not entering me, fucking me properly, makes me want to cry. "No! I'm on the pill." I have been since puberty. Not that there was any chance of getting pregnant in my solitude, but my father couldn't risk me having any offspring.

He chuckles, slowly removing his fingers from me. I gasp. He brings his lips to the shell of my ear. "There's so much you don't know about yourself. You control your fertility. Female Weres have the power to decide when they want to be pregnant. But so that you know, I'm tested annually even though I don't need to be. All this time, and I've been holding back for this."

Does that mean he's a virgin? I doubt it. Nothing about his skill suggests this is his first time. I don't let myself dwell on his words too long. I believe he's free of anything. I trust in his care for me, even though I shouldn't. He's the one to bring it up after all. I'm so naive, I'd let him fill me up even without any safeguards in place.

He positions his head at my entrance, barely applying force, but the pressure is already intense. "I can't wait to show you how strong you are. But first I need to break you, have you whimpering in my arms as I fill you." He thrusts inside of me, causing my world to spin. It's painful, but I'm so aroused that I welcome it, eager for more.

Ramblings pour from my lips as he continues to buck his way inside of me. One of his hands cups my breast and plays with my nipple while the other skims through my seam, causing obscene sounds of wetness.

"Fuck, you fit me so perfectly." His fangs push into my neck, and I arch into them. It's no wonder I'm addicted to pain. My life has been riddled with it, but this time it's my choice, and it's surrounded by so much pleasure that it turns the word into something else entirely. His fangs dig in deeper from my urging as he seats himself farther inside of me. "Oh, Grimm. It's so good. More."

He thrusts hard, and I scream. "So greedy. Don't worry, little fox. I'll give you everything." His control snaps, and he fucks me without caution, pounding into me as I cry out, a second orgasm washing over me with more urgency than the first. He roars as his speed breaks, and a warm liquid floods inside of me.

It's not over yet. An immense pressure builds at my entrance, stretching me wide. "Shit," Grimm murmurs. "Ember, I'm sorry."

"What?" I try to pull away to turn, but I'm stuck. I look over my shoulder instead, holding myself up against the wall and catching our bodies connected, the sight so erotic I almost come again.

"This has never happened before. I didn't know."

"Didn't know what?" There's no more pain. My body has grown used to the pressure.

His eyes catch mine, and his forehead crinkles. "My knot. I've never knotted anyone before. I didn't know that was possible for me."

"What's a knot?" I immediately regret the question because he's obviously horrified. He can't pull away, though. We're stuck, and he must answer me.

"The bulge at my base, that's what's holding us together. It's there to keep my seed inside of you."

"But you said I couldn't get pregnant." I'm on the pill, but my body feels completely full. I wonder if there's a limit.

"You can't, but my body will still do its damnedest. Ember, is this your first time?"

"With a knot?"

"With a man. Are you a virgin?"

I pop my ears and tails back in, feeling exposed—wild considering how intimate we are at the moment. "I've never been with another man."

"Oh, Ember. I'm so sorry." He slaps his face. "I should have known. I'm an idiot."

"Are you a virgin?"

He chuckles, but it's not cruel. "No, I'm not. I'm sorry, Ember. I wish I had made your first time more special." He picks me up, lying me on his office floor next to him, a tricky maneuver, but he accomplishes it seamlessly. He runs his human fingers through my hair. The touch soothes the self-conscious part of me.

I shrug. "It felt pretty special to me."

I hear his smile. He kisses my cheek. "It was special. Mind-fucking-blowing, but it doesn't have to be that rough. I can't imagine the pain that must have caused for your first time."

"I liked the pain. I'm used to it."

He tenses behind me. "I don't like that."

"Why?"

"I don't want you to be in pain."

"Sorry."

He pops free and rolls me over so I'm facing him. "I only want to bring you pleasure." He kisses my lips.

"I'll take both."

"I'll give you whatever you need." He pulls me against his chest, running his hand down my hair. I listen to his heartbeat. I've never listened to another person's. No one has ever hugged me this close, at least not that I remember. Somehow, this embrace feels even more intimate than everything else we've done. After weeks of uncertainty, my mind clears. I was wrong. My whole upbringing was wrong. This is good, and I want this to last. My mission has changed—for good.

16

GRIMM

My body begs for sleep. It's had its way. I've sated the primal urge that has raged throughout my system since she arrived, but my mind runs rampant. She was a virgin, of course she was. I should have known. Perhaps I surmised that, but once we began, I couldn't think clearly. Whenever I'm in her presence, my reason runs blank. The mental block previously drove me mad. Why couldn't I reason around her? But I don't need to question now. I know why.

She's my mate.

I knotted her.

Some Weres have a knot at all times, regardless of whether they have found their mate. Some only have it when they find their special match. I always thought I belonged to the second group, or more likely, the third, that would never knot at all. I'd had my fair share of serious relationships over the years. The fact that none of them were my mate didn't bother me much, but there was always something missing, always something I couldn't explain. I suspected I was the problem.

At my age, I should have been attuned to the signs, but I never honestly thought it would happen to me. Once I passed my thirties, I was sure I fell into that camp. I've heard from other Weres about how obvious it was when they found their missing piece. Cameron almost knew immediately when he happened upon Red in the woods. Maybe it's because Ember's Were-part is so muted. Of course, it's obvious to me now. How can I expect to be around her for another moment without covering her with kisses and pounding into her until she's full and can't remove herself from me?

My animal side only thinks of waking her in the mere moments of the night and having my way with her again, regardless of whether it's only been a few hours. My human side wants to keep my distance before talking to make sure this is what she really wants. She clearly just tasted freedom. Does she truly want to be shackled to an older man?

The warring pieces of me won't quiet down anytime soon. I rise from bed, heading into my home office to take care of the work I missed while fucking Ember against my office wall. I groan when I open my email and find never-ending red notifications. Most of them are news websites I set up to automatically notify me whenever something new about Weres comes out. I've been combing through, trying to gauge if it's from someone who's a serious threat to my pack.

I scroll through my inbox. All of these could be important, but I should actually get some sleep to be somewhat productive tomorrow, even if it's the weekend. I'll probably have to go to the kitchen and gulp down a sleeping pill. Honestly, checking my emails should be my assistant's job, but I'm finding it hard to give her any challenging tasks. Not that I don't trust her, I just want her to be spoiled and carefree. I would rather drown myself in tedious tasks than cause her even the slightest inconvenience.

One email catches my eye. It's from the DOS.

Minister Grimm,

Following a comprehensive review of the digital evidence provided, our Cybersecurity Division has completed an analysis of the transmitted footage and associated network data. The originating IP address has been identified as being associated with your primary office location.

Preliminary findings suggest that a substantial portion of video and social media activity originating from Dayton is being disseminated internally. Based on the available data, an individual within your organization is responsible for these transmissions.

Please be advised to initiate internal security protocols and personnel review procedures as appropriate. Our office will continue to monitor the situation and provide further updates as new information becomes available.

I read it three more times, just to make sure I'm not going crazy. How could the videos be coming from our headquarters? I've known my pack for most of my life. There'd be no reason for anyone to leak information that would put themselves and the people they love in danger. There can't be people hiding around the perimeter. We'd smell them. This doesn't make sense. My mind whirls through the faces of the members who spend time at the stone building, every person ringing more and more unlikely. Until I get to the last face, the newest addition. But it couldn't be. She's my mate.

My body and mind may be rewired from the mating bond, but a portion of my reason remains. Ember is the most likely suspect, but even still, I can't believe it's true.

17

EMBER

I don't know what I want.

It's Saturday, so I didn't expect Grimm to knock on my door to wake me for work, but I did expect him to come at some point in the day. It's hard not to feel rejected. Sure, last night, he cuddled me on his office floor for half an hour, cleaned me up, walked me home, and kissed me passionately. We didn't talk much after the sex. It wasn't awkward, though. At least it wasn't for me.

I may be naive, but I'm not dumb. I'm not supposed to act clingy just because we fucked. His words held promises I tucked into the freshly open corners of my heart, but a lust-filled passion could have just blinded him. Or, he's giving me my space. He was so apologetic when he learned I was a virgin. It gave me a boost of confidence that I wasn't obvious, but really, he did most of the work. It probably freaked him out, and he's worried I'll run away like I tend to do whenever I feel things are getting too heavy.

I spent the day reading—okay, mostly scrolling on my phone, but it was nice to just veg out for a bit. Even if I couldn't get Grimm out of my head, the relaxation made it even more difficult to do so. I wasn't completely useless. I texted Red in the morning and asked if he could meet up. Surprisingly, she invited me to come over this afternoon. Perfect for me, since I have nothing going on except obsessing over Grimm's thoughts. Perhaps she's craving some adult interaction after being bunkered in with a newborn.

I'm a jittery mess as I prepare to exit my cottage and go to Grimm's place to ask to use the car. But I don't have to travel too far because I find a note on my door.

Ember,

I'm so sorry I can't spend the day with you today. I still have a lot of work to catch up on, so I'll be in the office. I hope you get some rest. The car keys are under your mat in case you want to go into town.

Grimm

I reread the note three times, searching for a hidden meaning. He could still be avoiding me, but at least he's not ghosting me. I wonder when he put the note there. If only I had ventured outside earlier, I could have saved myself hours of unneeded pondering. I stuff the keys and note in my pocket and travel to the truck at the end of Grimm's driveway.

The trip should only take me a few minutes, but she couldn't give me an address to type into my GPS, only directions. I had to slow down multiple times to reread her text. After about twenty minutes, I pull into the long dirt driveway leading to her secluded cabin. She steps out onto her porch as I hop out of the truck. "Hey!"

"Hi," I reply, waving. "Thanks for having me over."

"Of course, I'm glad you reached out." She walks down the steps to greet me, wearing a black athleisure set with her bright red hair tied up into a high pony-tail. Damn her. I doubt I'd look as good after popping out a baby. I don't even look as good now.

"You ready?" she asks.

"Ready?" I had mentioned that I wanted help learning about my powers. I could have asked Grimm, but I need female companionship. Being in his presence would only end in us either bickering or wanting to fuck each other's brains out, and that wouldn't help me understand my skills in the least bit.

"To test out your abilities," she responds.

"Right, yes." I thought we'd sit down, have a cup of coffee first, but she's probably busy. It makes sense to get down to business.

She walks past me, turning so I can hear her. "There's a small clearing just past those trees. That should be a good place to start."

"Oh, I should tell you. I can't really *do* anything with my powers." My own secluded arena seems unnecessary.

She trots forward. "Not yet, but you never know what can happen when you try."

I jog up to her, embarrassed that I'm already out of breath after a few high-speed steps. "Where's the baby?" I ask once I catch up.

"Cameron's got her."

"Ah, makes sense."

"How are things going with Grimm?"

I tense. "What do you mean?"

She chuckles as she studies me. "I meant dealing with him as a boss and living in his guest house. It seemed tense the last time I saw you at the diner. But perhaps there's something else going on?"

"No." I rush the word out. You'd think I would be a better liar after pretending to be something I'm not for so long, but I can feel the lie spreading across my skin and spilling out of my eyes.

She throws her hands up. "You don't need to tell me anything."

I shake my head, accepting defeat. "No, you're right. There is something more going on." Yes, I wanted to come here to learn more about my powers, but also to talk to someone. Red knows Grimm better than I do. Perhaps she can shed light on my confusing situation.

"Are you okay?" She stops, touching my arm.

Red is a girl's girl. She barely knows me and seems willing to protect me. She's not much older than me, maybe a few years, but she appears much more capable. I'm glad to know I'd have her in my corner. "Yes, I'm fine. He's always respectful. I am just having a hard time reading him."

She nods. "Yeah, he's like that. Very serious most of the time. But he's a good guy. If you like him and he likes you, which I can tell he does, you shouldn't worry about your heart getting broken."

"Good to know." I smile at her just as she holds back a tree branch in our way, leading me into an opening, surrounded by tall trees.

"Okay, let's see what you can do," she says, taking a place at the center of the clearing.

"What? I already told you. I can't do anything."

"Let me see your transformation. I can turn around if you want to take your clothes off first."

"What?" I laugh. "Why would I take my clothes off?"

"Because some Weres clothes rip from their bodies when they transform."

"Oh, right." My mind rushes the night before in Grimm's office, his clothing falling to the floor in shreds around him. I hope she can't sense my blood heating. "I just get a tail and ears. It won't pop through my dress or anything, just fall from the bottom."

"That's more than me."

"Really?"

"Yeah, I don't have any physical transformations except the glowing eyes and claws."

"Then what makes you a Were?" I tense, nervous my question was rude.

She shrugs, walking in a circle. "Well, my dad was half werewolf, so mostly that, but I have abilities. I'm able to control minds." She wiggles her fingers and smiles as if revealing a spooky story.

"Really?"

"Sort of. For a short amount of time when I'm in the person's presence."

"Wow." If the Hunters harnessed that kind of power, Weres would be fucked.

"Good thing I'm not evil, right?" It's comforting to hear she doesn't view herself as evil, despite what the Hunters have drilled into my head for my entire life. The question is, do I believe her? I don't think Grimm is evil, so why not her? It makes my stomach churn that all my beliefs are changing so suddenly.

She laughs. "I can also cause earthquakes."

"Are you being for real?"

"I swear! Being a werewolf is pretty cool, and everyone has a different experience. I didn't even know I was a Were until recently, when I met Cameron."

"How did you not know?"

"Mine are so subtle. Besides, I think finding my mate helped bring my powers to the surface."

"Your mate?"

She sighs. "Yeah, it sounds kind of weird, but Weres have predestined partners." Her eyes grow wide, as if remembering something. "Not all Weres. I've met a lot of couples that aren't with a fated mate but still are completely happy in their relationship."

"How do you know you found your mate?"

"Everyone's different. Knots are usually involved, but it's also a feeling, a connection. Full Weres are better at realizing it."

Knots. That's what Grimm mentioned the night before, but no, it couldn't be... "What's a knot?"

Her cheeks blush and her eyes dart nervously as she chuckles. "It's part of the male's junk."

"In what way?"

"Ugh, this is so weird." She laughs. "It's like another ballsack at the base that gets hard after they, ya know, finish."

"So it only gets hard when males find their mates?"

"Apparently not. Some males always have it."

That must be the case for Grimm, but didn't he say he's never done that before? I can't remember. I could have imagined it. No point in getting my thoughts wrapped in a twist. He's not my mate. That's not possible. And even if it is, it's the least of my concerns right now.

Red shakes her head. "Okay, let's get back to business. Show me what you got." She rubs her hands together.

"I'd rather talk about ballsacks."

She bursts into laughter. "Oh come on! I just told you I barely have any Were abilities. You're in good company."

"You can control minds!"

"So?"

"That's like the coolest superpower. I just have a bushy tail."

"Aw, it sounds cute."

"It's disgusting." I look at the ground, the light-heartedness of the conversation fading. Tears prick at the corner of my eyes.

Red's footsteps crunch closer to me, and she places her hand on my shoulder. "Hey, it's okay. Whatever form you take won't bother me, and maybe I can help you learn how to appreciate yourself more."

It's so odd. Red and Grimm both talk about my otherness in such a way that is so foreign to me. They make it seem so easy to believe, and perhaps, the effortlessness of their ideas is rubbing off on me. I nod. "I don't know if I can just make myself shift. My whole life, I've been taught to hide it, and whenever it did poke through, it was because of something outside of my control."

Red taps her full lips. "I have an idea, but you might not like it."

"What is it?"

"What if I made you shift?"

"Like scare me?"

"No, like go into your mind."

I back away, shaking my hands in front of me. "I don't know about that."

"It's okay. You don't have to. I just thought I'd offer. It seems you have mental blocks that I could help with, but obviously, it's invasive. We don't have to train today. We can go back to my place, and I'll make us coffee. There will be a screaming baby present, but just ignore her."

When I arrived, chatting over a cup of coffee seemed perfect, and that should be the case now, but a piece of me doesn't want to leave. Red's abilities scare me, but perhaps it could be a key to revealing a version of myself I've never known. The last few weeks have been spent dealing with parts of myself that are foreign and intimidating. What's one more thing?

"No, I think I want you to."

"Are you sure?"

"Is it dangerous?"

"No. I've helped regain my granny's memories. She barely noticed when it was happening, and it's helped her tremendously. We can always stop if you're uncomfortable."

I nod, wanting to speed this up so I don't think my way out of it. "Okay, let's do this."

She steps in front of me, only a few inches separate us. "Okay, I'm going in." Her eyes turn blazing gold.

I take a step back, but straighten when nothing happens. "What's happening?"

"I'm just working on digging through some of your mental blocks. Okay, try to transform."

Maybe she's crazy. There still must be conspiracy theories even in a paranormal community. Perhaps she just thinks she's controlling minds, because I don't feel anything.

Despite my skepticism, I attempt to tell myself to shift mentally.

I gasp. It's never happened like this. My eyes burn. Ears grow from my scalp, and my tail brushes against the back of my leg under my dress. Something is different this time, though—a tingling at my fingertips. I bring my hands to my face, examining my claws. Burnt orange fur lines my razor-sharp nails and spreads down my fingers. "Oh, my God."

"Well, that's cool as fuck," Red says, smiling at me.

"I've never grown claws before," I say in awe.

Red jumps, pumping a fist in the air. "Hell ya! Two bad bitches using their powers and shit."

I roll my eyes, despite my smile, and outstretch my arms to examine my new self. It's weird—for the first time in my life, my Were-form doesn't repulse me. In fact, I kind of like it.

It's obvious now. I'm not a Hunter. I'm a Were, and maybe it's time I do something to right all the wrongs I've done against my people.

18

GRIMM

I've ransacked the office. Not just Ember's, everyone's. Although Ember, logically, is the most probable suspect, I could leave no stone unturned. I still can't bring myself to believe she would do this. I even went through my own office, wondering if I've been bugged.

After about four hours and finding nothing, I decide I need to talk to someone I trust. Perhaps with the new insight, they could help me reason. Cameron comes to mind. He's already dealing with so much, but he's still the Human Liaison. He's accustomed to the high-stakes responsibilities. He'll know what to do.

I call him, cringing once he answers, and crying ensues in the background.

"Hey, what's up?" he says, casual as ever.

"Is this a bad time?"

"No, I'm good. What's up?" A door opens, and then silence.

"I heard back from the DOS. They traced the IP address from most of the videos that came from Dayton. They're being posted from the office."

"Shit."

"Yeah."

"Who do you think it could be?"

I'm silent for a moment.

He breaks it, "You don't think..."

"I don't know what else to think. It doesn't make sense to be anyone else. The entire pack has been with us since they were children."

"Do you think she's dangerous? She's about to come here to meet with Red?"

An idea pops into my mind.

"No, I don't think she is, but even so, Red can handle herself."

"Should I tell her?"

"No, keep this between us—at least, if you're comfortable with that. It's good Ember is making friends, and I don't want to assume anything until I've discovered evidence." It's a risky suggestion, putting Red, someone I care about, in the line of danger, but despite what logic tells me, I still can't believe Ember—my mate—would do this.

"Okay. Keep me updated, and I'll let you know if I catch anything suspicious."

"Thanks."

We hang up, and I know exactly what I need to do. I leave the office, not exiting the woods but hanging by the treeline, watching Ember's cottage. The sun sits low in the sky when she finally opens her front door, reads the note I left for her this morning, and grabs the keys from under the mat.

I stalk closer, waiting until the truck completely disappears down the driveway, and then a few minutes after that, before I walk up the steps of her front porch. She left the door open. It comforts me. If she's a criminal mastermind, locking away her secrets would be on the top of her mind, but perhaps she's grown too comfortable. I know I have up until this point.

I step inside, the scent of her encapsulating me and making my knees weak. The primal part of me wants to lie in her unmade sheets, bring her pillow up to my nose, and take himself in hand. A day without her near has been too much. I can't think properly. Of course, I haven't been able to reason since she crashed into my life, but now that I know she's my mate, the urges I feel for her take all my senses, making them even stronger.

I clench my fists, grounding myself to focus on where to search first. Perhaps her underwear drawer? *Fuck. No.* Just when I'm about to yank one out to get it over with, her laptop on the desk in the corner catches my eye. Obviously, this would be the best place to look. I sit down, opening the device, expecting to find a password-protected lockscreen, and yet it's free for me to scroll through. Damn is she trusting, making everything I'm doing right now seem even more fucked up.

Her desktop is organized, with very few applications, and features a sunset as her background. I click through her folders, looking half-heartedly for anything that could make sense. I find a photo album. It's mostly photos she's taken of herself from her childhood. It's invasive, but the moment I catch a snapshot of those big green eyes, I can't look away.

I don't even realize hours have passed until I've reached the last photo. Shame washes over me. I didn't catch anything vulnerable, but I could have stumbled upon something completely inappropriate for me to see. The images made me realize just how lonely Ember's life must have been up to this point. None of them featured any friends or family; they were just pictures of herself, animals, or the nature around her. It's like she wanted to document her life. Despite the way she was mistreated and told to hate her powers, she refused to disappear in her own, silent fight. My heart aches for her, even if reason pounds at my mental door.

Ember has experienced abuse and neglect throughout her lifetime. She feels ashamed of her werewolf abilities, which means her family rejected that part of herself. It would make sense that she would be a Hunter—they would treat their children in such a way, breeding for our powers, but still repulsed by our nature. Despite not finding anything yet, the truth seems glaring. How could I not put these pieces together sooner—right when she revealed parts of her unsettling past? Perhaps I was blinded by the mating bond. Perhaps I still am.

Just when I'm about to leave, take a cold shower, and admit everything I've done to Ember in the morning. A file titled *Dayton Weres* catches my eye. My finger hovers over the cursor for much too long before I can't take it anymore and click in. It's video files. I open the first one, immediately recognizing it. It's a young man alone in the woods, shifting into his Were-form. The recorder hides behind trees as they record. When I saw this video online weeks before, I wondered how the person managed to keep their scent hidden. Of course, Ember would be able to do this, perhaps without even realizing she could. Foxes are known for their stealth in the animal kingdom. Despite my constant awareness of her scent, she might not be detectable to someone who's not her mate.

The Were runs off into the distance, and the video ends. I click through more, so many more. Half of them have been uploaded, so a small, wishful part of me chooses to believe she could have just downloaded these videos. Perhaps she was compiling them to help us stop whoever took them. That thought is quickly squashed once I realize half of the videos haven't been posted yet. *She took these.*

All the videos feature people—my people—transforming into their Were-forms without anyone noticing. Some are young—teenagers, while some are the eldest in our community. Everyone stands to become vulnerable if all of these are released. I select all of the videos—something like twenty—and delete them, clearing out her trash bin as well. It's not the solution. She probably has the original videos on her phone. She just stored them here for easier upload when she's ready to post them.

I'm raw, broken. There's no way to deny the evidence previously in front of me. Ember is the bug. She's a Hunter, set on destroying the people I love most. I should hate her, come up with a plan to dispose of her, yet my mind only shuffles through the images of her—alone, naive. I need to clear my head.

I stand. Night has fallen without my noticing. Something shuffles outside the front door, boots wiping the front mat. My instincts kick in, and my eyes find the half-open closet in Ember's room. I sprint, using my wolf abilities to move quickly and without a sound. I shouldn't be hiding. I should confront Ember about what I found, hold her hostage, and contact the DOS, but I can't bring myself to do that yet. I still don't know what I'm going to do with her.

She enters with a sigh, throwing a tote bag onto the counter by the front door and padding to the bedroom. I sink deeper into her hung-up clothing, wondering if she can sense me the way I can her. It doesn't seem like an ability she has, but we're mates and we bonded, her powers will grow.

The shower turns on, and she bangs around in the bathroom next to the closet. *She's naked.* Images of her breasts in my hand, my tongue running through her cunt wash my mind of reason. I need her. My cock aches in my slacks. Perhaps I could jack off to settle myself, but I fight my urges. I've already gone through her personal belongings and am hiding in her closet. Coming over her clothing is another line of inappropriate, although it shouldn't matter. I can't be with her after everything I found.

My lust turns into anger. How could she do this to me? Surely she doesn't know she's my mate, but she must sense something stronger than attraction. She stands just on the other side of the thin walls, planning my demise yet radiating a scent I can't ignore. My days will be filled with nothing but turmoil. I can never have her again, yet I won't be able to live without her. I want to punish her, to sink my teeth in her flesh and make her feel even a fraction of the pain she'll cause me for the rest of my sorry, miserable life. It's almost like that dream so many nights before was a premonition. Perhaps I was meant to devour her—be the monster she views me as.

I wait, my mind ruminating over my hazy rage. The water turns off, and moments later, the bathroom door opens. I'm eager for her to stumble upon me, for her to scream in terror once she finds me hidden. I bet a shiver of arousal will pass through her before I destroy her. The thought stiffens my cock further. A small piece of myself yells in the distance, urging me to stop, to get out of here and give myself space to think clearly, but his screams grow further away as more of her wafts through my nostrils. Her cunt is bare just outside the closet door. It's so close for the taking.

The thin line of light under the door flickers out, and the bed creaks under her weight. She's completely unaware of my presence as she begins her descent into slumber. I wait until her breath evens. It maddens me more that she can fall asleep so easily. Her mind doesn't war with the decisions she's made. She has no qualms with her choices. How could my fated mate be so evil?

When I'm nearly certain she's asleep, I creep out of her closet, scanning just to make sure. The moonlight from the open window illuminates her splayed amongst her white sheets, a pillow between her legs, and one perfect curve of her bare ass presented before me. She sleeps in the nude. The smell overpowers me. Even if I weren't standing above her and were snug in my bed across the lake, surely I'd be able to smell her.

I have no plans as I climb onto the foot of the bed, anger and desire still taking turns as the controller of my emotions. She startles slightly as I grow closer, but her eyes don't flutter open until I'm hovering over her. Her body is still damp from her shower, and her wet hair weighs heavily against her scalp. My mind can't recognize the wetness as a result of her shower, all it pictures is her covered in sweat from the exertion of riding me, screaming around the girth of my knot.

"Grimm?" Her voice is hoarse, and she flutters her long eyelashes as she takes me in. I snap my hand over her mouth, attempting to cut off more words. I can't think clearly when she speaks, her voice so soft and sweet, promising nothing but pleasure, but only delivering pain.

Her eyes grow in panic, and she wriggles underneath my weight. "I went through your computer. I know what you are, what you've been doing."

She slackens at my words and nods under my furry hand, shifting involuntarily. My claws poke at the tender flesh of her cheeks. Tears welled in her eyes, the sight softening me slightly.

"Ember, how could you do this to me? To us? You are a Were as well."

She nods, and her hand attempts to grip around my wrist; the other hand runs softly down my forearm.

I look away from her, clenching my eyes. "Fuck!" I yell into the darkness. "I shouldn't want you this badly. I should want to kill you, become the monster you view me as." Her breath heaves under my hand as my cock strains against my slacks and into her bare midsection.

Her arousal hits me like a bullet, causing my head to spin. I turn back to her, her eyelids growing heavy. "You want me, little fox. Your cunt begs for me, even if you want to see me dead." I shake my head, bringing my lips to her ear. "I should punish you, make you beg for it, have you choking around my cock until I spill my dirty seed down your throat." I lick her temple, trailing down her neck. "I should keep you as my prisoner, lock you up until you're rid of your birth control, filling you with my seed every day until you're full of my dirty werewolf offspring." I release my grip from her mouth as I hover over her pebbled nipples. She moans, arching her breaths into my mouth. "You dirty fox. You'd like that, wouldn't you?"

I bit her nipple, causing her to scream. "Please, Grimm."

I lap the valley between her breasts, grinding my hardened length against her exposed lips. "Please what? Please don't kill you? Please fuck you?" I pause, holding myself over her as I study her. I'm not in my right state of mind, but still, she's my mate. I don't want to hurt her, as much as another part of me does

"Do with me as you please," she says, arching her neck and meeting her lips to mine. She kisses me with an open mouth and a frantic tongue, hot and wanting. I return her vigor, tasting her as if it is the last time, because it very well is.

I jolt upright, unbuttoning my shirt and releasing myself from my pants. I watch her as I remove my clothes, emotions welling in my chest. She's so beauti-ful, ethereal under the light of the moon, wrapped in white sheets, her silver hair glowing beneath her damp frame.

"I can't look at you," I grunt angrily, swooping her in my arms and flipping her around so her ass presses against my cock. I fold over her, my dick pushing through velvet as one hand grips around her neck and the other trails underneath her. I grab her breast, and she bucks into me. "You want me to fuck you like this? Eager for my monster cock splitting you in two?"

"Yes, please!"

I pinch her nipple, causing her to cry out, but my other hand applies pressure to her neck, straining the feral sounds escaping her. "I could teach you so much. I could strum your body every which way, show you what true pleasure feels like." I travel lower, teasing my finger along her curls. "You greedy little thing, letting me play with you as you plan my demise." My words incite my anger, and instead of dipping my fingers into her and wringing her of her pleasure, I angle my cock at her entrance, pushing into her without caution.

She cries out, surely from pain but also drawing in pleasure.

"I should fuck you senseless," I drone, increasing my speed and losing myself even more. "I should fill you, rip you in half, and leave you for someone else to clean up." My body fills with a warm lava, but even in my rage, I can't leave her without her pleasure. I squeeze her breast with one hand and with the other I part her lips, seeking out her swollen bundle of nerves.

"Oh, fuck, Grimm. So good!" she cries as I don't let up my force, using her, but also growing closer to my edge at the thought of her lost in her pleasure.

My emotions tumble around each other, part of me wanting this to be good for her. Part of me re-alizes that's selfish. It only makes me harder to hear her scream my name. I want to ruin her, make her understand what she's done. No time to unravel my thoughts, only fuck my mate as she screams out from under me.

She comes quickly, beautifully. I hold her body as her knees give out and she convulses underneath me. Yes, I want to fill her with my seed, but I don't want to be stuck to her after this. I pull out at the last moment, and she falls to the mattress underneath us. I work my length with two rough tugs before I erupt, spraying her back with my hot seed. I watch in satisfaction as I coat her, wondering if she's repulsed by me. Only the day before I filled her with my cum, had her begging for it, but I'll never be sure if it was all an act.

I crawl off the bed once I release my last drop, unable to look at her as I quickly pull my clothes on. From the corner of my eye, I can see her sit up and cover herself with her sheets. It's silent, the only sound is me rushing my buttons.

"I'm sorry, Grimm," she whispers, tremors in her voice.

"Leave in the morning. Take the truck. Get far away." I finally look at her. One last time.

She nods, tears running down my cheeks. Yes, I must tell the pack, reveal that I let someone in who was dangerous. It won't be the first time I've let my guard down and put people at risk. I should want to see justice, to have her pay for her crimes, but I can't. She's still my mate—always will be. I burn her image into my memory before turning and walking out the door.

19

EMBER

I did it. Something I should have done a long time ago. And even after last night, I don't regret it.

I haven't stopped crying since Grimm left. I should have explained things and told him I'd already made it right, but I don't deserve his forgiveness. I don't deserve him. One measly post can't erase everything I've done.

You'd think my tears would dry out by now, but as I stuff the rest of my clothing into my duffel bag, they still flow. I don't want to leave. I'm finally in a place where I can learn about my powers and am surrounded by people like me. But more than that, I don't want to be without Grimm.

I've never been in a relationship before, so as far as I know, breakups always feel this painful. How can people survive this time and time again? I don't think I'll make it past the Dayton limits without my heart bursting from my chest. Is this love, or just a sort of obsession? It feels powerful, burrowed into every strand of my DNA. Perhaps the intense feelings just confirm how naive and inexperienced I am. We've known each other for such a short amount of time. It shouldn't be this big of a deal.

When I packed my bags to leave my childhood home—the prison that disguised itself as safety—I moved swiftly, not taking time to wallow in my emotions or contemplate whether I was making the right decision. Now, I stall. I don't have many belongings. Everything in the kitchen, all the linens, the decor, all of it belongs to Grimm. I just have my clothes and toiletry items. It shouldn't take several hours to pack.

I started before sunrise, sure that if I didn't leave soon, someone would break down my door and escort me off to werewolf prison for my crimes. But now the morning is bright, and no one has come for me.

Perhaps I want to be carted off. If that happens, I don't have to think about where I'll head next.

I sit at the edge of my bed, which is still disheveled, covered in remnants of Grimm. I stare at the mess I wiped from my back, wondering if I should pack the dirty sheets with me. It seems disgusting, but I want every piece of him. He thinks he repulses me. How could I let him leave without telling him how badly it hurt to have him not fill me completely? Everything about him is intoxicating. I can hate myself for being a Were, but never him, even when I tried my hardest.

I should leave a note, explain everything, but if I did, I'd risk him following me, and I don't deserve that—not after lying to him and putting him and his pack in so much danger. Sure, hating werewolves—myself—was all I knew. I didn't get to pick the family I was raised in, but still, the actions were my own. After the video I posted last night in Red's driveway before returning to my cottage—well, not my cottage anymore—I hope that there's a more equal playing field. I doubt the video will do much, but hopefully, it'll help ease some of the negative exposure I caused.

The front door creaks open, and my heart races. I jump to my feet, reaching for the bedroom doorknob and throwing myself out into the living space. I expect Grimm. It could be anyone coming for me, but I can't help that I hope he changed his mind, even though I don't deserve that. The man standing in the entrance-way, shutting the door behind him, isn't Grimm, not even close.

"Father?" Confusion comes before fear.

"Ember," he replies, his expression void of joy as he walks closer to me.

I've always been eager for my father's love, even if he didn't deserve it. I wanted nothing more than to please him. It's the reason I came to Dayton. I went through his office, finding the files containing information on the various werewolf packs. For some reason, Dayton stood out to me. He never let me be part of the Hunters. I wasn't bred to fight. He's an important man. Having a part-Were daughter would bring nothing but embarrassment. Instead, he kept me locked away, where no one could find his dark secret—told me I was lucky he cared too much about me to discard me. I believed it too. I ran away to show him just how capable I was. I could expose the werewolves, show the world how disgusting they truly were, but I was wrong about everything. Perhaps I'm wrong about him, too.

"What are you doing here?" I ask, dripping fear. This can't be good, not after what I posted last night.

"I think you know why I'm here, Ember." He walks closer as I back away, catching the flicker of anger in his green eyes—just like mine, but now I see there's no similarity between us except the color. "I debated coming after you sooner. I worried about what you would do considering your nature. No matter how obedient you'd been throughout your life, you'd always be part monster. You were never too bright. You're still on my phone bill, daughter. It was easy to find where you'd run off to. It was interesting at first, but then we tracked the IP address from the latest videos, and I put the pieces together. You were exposing the Weres here in Dayton. You were doing this to prove you could be a Hunter. I was proud."

For a moment, the flicker of the feeling flashes across his features, the first time I've ever witnessed it. It's gone as quickly as it came. "But then, after last night, when you posted those private family videos." He shakes his head. "We had the public in our hands, and you showed them something without context, making them doubt the intentions of the Hunters."

I'm eager to check the comments on my video. Could it have reached enough people to make a dent in the public perception so soon? Or is he just predicting the inevitable? "Good!" I yell, finding my rage. "You tortured me. My whole life, I was abused just because of the way that I was born."

"I did what I did to protect you."

"No!" I yell. "You were afraid of me. You wanted my powers for yourself and punished me for being stronger than you."

He turns his head, clenching his teeth. I hit a nerve. He obviously doesn't have a rebuttal. "Such a short time away, and you're obviously brainwashed. Playtime is over. You've forgotten yourself, and it's time to come back home."

"No!" I yell, shocked at the strength in my voice. I've never spoken to him this way.

He laughs, void of humor. "No?"

"I'm not leaving."

He nods, looking around the small room. "Do you know whose property you're staying on?" He doesn't let me answer. "Ah, but of course you do. Not only are you living with a werewolf, but the Minister of the Dayton werewolf pack. Did you let him get to you? I imagine it wouldn't be difficult. He'd have to show you just an ounce of attention, and you'd give over every part of yourself." He shakes his head. "Just like your mother."

I ball my fists. I never knew her, but still, the loyalty I feel for her runs deep.

He chuckles again, his green eyes wild. "I'm right, aren't I? You've gone soft and betrayed your family because you're fucking a monster, aren't you?"

My cheeks redden, despite my attempts to mask my emotions.

His expression shifts, red cheeks, furrowed brows, and balled fists clenched at his side. "You'd better have taken your birth control. We'll have to clean every inch of you when you get home. I can practically smell the rot wafting off of you." He lunges for me, grabbing my wrist and yanking me toward him. I scream, bloodcurdling.

"Enough," he yells. "You're lucky it's me fetching you and not another member of the Hunters. They would drag you out of here with far more bruises. Perhaps even dead."

"I'm not going back with you! You lied to me. They're not monsters. I'm not a monster. You are. Even if you kill us all, it won't make you more of a man. You'll always be pathetic." I spit at the side of his face.

His grip lessens, staring at me with wide eyes before slapping me across the face.

The sound rings in my ear, twisting with the pain. I cup my cheek, blood already pooling in my mouth. Something lights in my veins, a trickle of power, similar to the feeling Red pulled from my mind, but it's not strong enough to grasp on my own.

"Let's go!" my father yells, pulling me by the wrist even as I drop to the floor to make it more difficult for him. I'm pathetic. I boasted to him about my powers, and yet, when I need them most, I'm unable to summon my strength. Father struggles with my weight for a moment before grunting and picking me up and throwing me over his shoulder. Before he can get far, the door flies open.

"Senator Green?" Grimm growls, his voice pure violence. "What the fuck are you doing here, and what are you doing with her?"

I fight to twist over my father's shoulder and see Grimm's expression, but my father just plops me to the ground with a laugh. "Minister Grimm, pleasure to see you. I'm just coming to retrieve what's mine."

I watch the two men, my emotions warring. Will I survive the heartbreak if Grimm steps to the side as my father carts me off? But of course, I shouldn't expect anything else, not after what I've done.

Grimm's face pinches in confusion, his fists balled at his side. "Yours?"

My father laughs. "You can't see the resemblance? Perhaps her deformed genetics take over what I've passed on." He sighs. "Yes, she is my daughter."

Grimm's eyes grow wide. "Your daughter?"

"Yes, and it seems she's been able to pull one over on you. Get you to cover room and board while she takes your pack down from the inside." He turns to me. "I guess she's not always a disappointment."

"No!" I yell. "It's not like that!"

Grimm studies me, his expression wounded.

"I hope she was worth it in the bedroom, Minister, but your time fucking my daughter has come to an end. I'm taking her with me, and we'll be out of your hair."

"No!" I'm shocked when Grimm and I say the word at the same time.

"No?" My father questions Grimm. "Don't you see what was going on? She didn't want you, you old bastard. She was just pretending to like you so she could expose your pack. She's been working for me this whole time."

"That's not true!" I yell through a sob. Most of it is, but it's different now. It's been different for a while.

"Leave her with me," Grimm says, stepping fully in my father's path.

"So you can dispose of her yourself? Tempting, but I have far better plans for her." He grabs my arm and tugs me forward. "No!" I yell again.

Grimm presses a hand against my father's chest. "She doesn't want to go with you."

"Why do you care? She fucked you over."

"Regardless of her actions, I know she's a good person and just raised by an evil man who doesn't see how special she is." Every part of me wants to weep. No one has ever spoken for me with such kindness. I'm obsessed with this man. I'd do anything to make him mine. I can't believe I was about to leave, to accept a life without him.

My father scoffs, rolling his eyes. "So you saw the new video, and you think you know everything about how I raised my daughter."

"What video?" Grimm asks. The question shocks me. He's choosing to keep me, even though he doesn't know I've tried to make amends. I'm sure I'm dreaming.

My father laughs again, pulling his phone out of his pocket. "Got it, so you're just a fucking idiot. I guess you all are." He types something and presses send. "Step to the side."

Grimm shifts, not entirely; his body is still human but covered with hair, tipped with claws and fangs, his clothes nearly bursting off him. "Leave her," he growls.

I'd expect my father to be frightened. He's been a Hunter all his life, but never actually seen combat, at least as far as I know. He entered politics early, working in secret and creating policies that helped the Hunters thrive. But my father doesn't seem the least bit threatened. He stares at Grimm with a cocky grin, and I wonder if he's hiding a weapon on him, the thought making me panic.

Grimm must also notice my father's strange confidence. He jolts the distance, grabbing my father and bringing him to the ground. "Go!" he yells, bringing his eyes to mine for just a moment.

I don't want to leave, but I know I'd just make it more difficult if I stay. I step to leave, but before I make any headway, a man barges into the cottage. It's Roland, my father's driver, wearing a black suit and sunglasses as usual. He points a pistol at Grimm's back.

"No!" I yell. "Don't!" Without a second thought, I step in front of the gun. Perhaps I'm confident, Roland, someone who has known me my whole life, wouldn't hurt me, but more likely, I must stop him from harming the other half of my soul. I can't live without Grimm—it's so clear to me now.

Roland only hesitates for a moment before cocking the gun, still aimed at my head.

"No!" Grimm shouts. I can't see him, but from my father's chuckle and steps reaching closer to me, I imagine Grimm got off of him at the chance of saving my life. My father's hand wraps around my wrist, pulling me to him. Roland snaps the gun back to Grimm behind me.

"Please!" I yell. "I'll go with you." I turn to my father, attempting to read him, to show him my desperation.

"Of course you're coming with me, but I'm not making deals with you."

I already know the next words out of his mouth, and if he says them, it's too late. My reasoning washes blank, and I act purely on instinct—not even having to summon anything within me. My claws eject from my hands, and I swipe the pointed tips across my father's throat. Blood gushes from the wound before he registers what happens.

My mind catches up as I watch the color drain from my father's face. Roland screams from behind me, and a body drops to the floor, followed by the clanking of the gun. I don't have to turn to find out what happened; I don't have to check with Grimm to see if he dealt with the threat. Everything is instinctual. We're safe, finally free. I know this for certain as I watch my father drop to his knees, dying before my eyes, at my hands.

20

GRIMM

There's not much worse than seeing your mate splattered with blood. It's not her own, but it doesn't make the sight any less unsettling. Ember can't stop shaking, her eyes wide and emotionless. She sits on the rocking chair on the porch overlooking the lake. It will probably be the last time she captures the view from this angle, as I can't imagine she'll want to be back at the home where she killed her father.

I haven't left her side, rubbing her back covered in the white quilt I snatched from the couch. We haven't spoken besides the urgent checking on each other's well-being after slaying the two intruders. I brought her out here and called Brick, quickly filling him in on what happened over the phone. It took less than thirty minutes before police cars and helicopters littered my yard.

Two stretchers exit the cabin, and I attempt to step in Ember's peripheral so she doesn't see her father's lifeless body rolled away. It's no use, though. Once they clank down the steps and down the pebbled pathway toward the ambulance, she sobs, resting her face in her hands. I kneel, shushing her in a way of soothing. I don't have words.

Of course, I think she did the right thing. If she didn't kill Senator Green and cause the distraction for me to overpower the gunman, both of us might be dead or worse. She didn't have any other choice. I doubt it will be easy for her to see it that way. She lived a life riddled with abuse, but he was still her father. Those bonds run deep. I don't know if she'll ever heal, but I know I must do my best to help. I can't believe that only yesterday I planned to have her out of my life for good. What was I thinking? She could stab me through the heart, and it would be a death worth dying.

Brick caught me up to speed about the video Ember posted last night when I called him to tell him that Senator Green lay lifeless on my guest house floor. With everything going on, it shouldn't have mattered, but I had to ask. He told me it was posted yesterday in the early evening. After some mental math, I realized it was before I confronted her. She betrayed her own father and the Hunters, well before she knew I knew. Not that it matters—she could be evil to the bone, and I don't think I'd be able to let her go.

"Grimm," Brick calls from the bottom step, motioning for me to come to him.

"I'll be right back," I whisper to Ember, before studying her and walking toward Brick.

"How's she doing?" he asks once I'm close enough.

"I don't know."

"Can't be easy killing your own father, even if he was an evil psychopath." We both watch her. She's stopped crying and has returned to staring out over the lake.

"She didn't have much time to contemplate. It happened so quickly. I think she was purely working on instincts."

"Hey, I don't blame her. I can't imagine growing up as a Were in a household run by Senator Green. Must've been torture."

I nod, my heart growing heavy. "Now what? It's not gonna be easy to cover this one up." This isn't like the last time we disposed of the Hunters, when Brick and Carmen killed the spy who ran the secret science torture facility. This is a senator. We suspected that the true leader of the Hunters was someone in power. People will miss him, not even just the Hunters. I'm still trying to wrap my head around the fact that the leader of the Hunters was my mate's father.

Brick sighs, and I study him—large bags under his eyes and heavyset shoulders. I wonder if there's more going on, besides all this fucked-up shit. "You know how the DOS is, it won't be easy, but they'll find a way to cover this. Hell, with the injuries, I bet they could even say it was self-inflicted due to the video that was released."

His words comfort me. They make sense. I scan around the property, peppered with police officers and brown-suited men chatting, typing on their phones, and looking through paperwork. These people are all meticulously selected by the higher-ups.

This isn't my first rodeo. Death seems to follow my pack. It's always out of self-defense, but it doesn't make it less imperative to hide the true details of the murders. If the truth were revealed, all that would follow would be court cases and my people being put at more risk for retaliation from the Hunters.

"Do you think this is the end?" Brick asks.

I pondered his question, returning my attention to Ember, still statuelike in the rocking chair. All I've ever known was hiding from the Hunters, even before I took the position as Minister. Although it's always been my goal to end the terror inflicted on my people, I don't think a part of me has truly thought it was possible. Could my mate be the end of all of this? It seems unlikely, but the more I think about it, the more I see the potential. Of course, there could be other members of the government that are tied to the Hunter organization, but if the DOS frames the Senator's death as a suicide because of the videos circulating that highlighted his abuse of young Weres, then it would be hard for the Hunters to publicly, or privately, continue their reign of terror. We wouldn't have to hide in the shadows. We could go public because, obviously, given the backlash to Ember's latest video, they have sympathy for us.

A pang of guilt vibrates through me. Could this have been the answer all along—showing the world who we are and what we suffer from? Being a leader always comes with guilt, but how will I ever grapple with the fact that I could have saved so many of my pack members if I only thought differently—like Carmen, like Ember?

As if the thought summoned her, another car pulls into view, parking in front of my guest house. Carmen steps out of the driver's seat.

"I bet she's relieved," I say. Of course, all werewolves should be relieved. The Hunter leader is dead, but Carmen carried a lot of guilt for the response to her exposure.

"You have no idea the turmoil she's been feeling since she posted that article," Brick says with a sigh.

"I have an idea." My heart grows heavy as I glance at Ember, my mate, who took a similar course of action to save my people and me.

Brick slaps my shoulder. "Look at us, both of our mates, causing havoc and doing what we should've done a long time ago."

I turned to him, wide-eyed. "Is it that obvious?" I haven't even uttered the words out loud, let alone to another person. Hearing Ember referred to as my mate coming from someone else's mouth tethers another part of me to her.

Brick clenched his teeth. "Oops, I wasn't supposed to say anything. That's just what Carmen and I theorized."

I chuckle, rolling my eyes. "Just keep this between you and me. I don't think Ember knows yet, and I don't want to tell her at this moment."

"Hey, if we're sharing secrets, I'll give you one of mine. Carmen's pregnant."

Shock comes before happiness. I hug him, overwhelmed by excitement, but quickly realize it's out of place and pull back. "Shit, man. That happened fast!"

"You're telling me." He smiles. "I guess that's what the knots are for." He glances out at his mate across the green, giving her a knowing smile. She huffs, rolling her shoulders back but clear happiness radiates off her face.

"You'll have to excuse me. I have a mate who needs to be attended to. Don't worry about this mess. We've got it. Take your mate home and make sure she's okay." He steps away, placing a hand on my shoulder before he turns.

I'm left alone, only a few feet separating Ember from me, but it might as well be an entire universe. How will I make her whole after everything she's been through? I watch her, the sunlight catching in her hair, the lapping water dancing in her eyes, sadness coating every inch of her skin. Perhaps I'll never fix her, repair the jagged edges of herself, but it doesn't matter to me. All I need is her, even if she's broken, even if she can only give me her scraps.

21

EMBER

For a moment, when awareness tickles the edges of my sleep and the warm bed drags me deeper, I'm at peace. I don't open my eyes, letting his smell soak into my pores. How can I make him out so clearly? It's like I see his face in the back of my mind the moment his fragrance meets my nostrils. It's not something I can name or describe, just an essence that's all him. I want to drown in it, but as sunlight breaks through the thin skin of my eyelids, I'm forced to face reality. The memories from the day before crash around me. Yes, I'm in Grimm's bed, a place I long to be, but the circumstances for my nest are from nothing but pain.

Grimm carried me here when I couldn't get my legs to walk the distance from my cottage to his house. I guess it's not *my* cottage. It never really was, but even more so now. I can't return, not after everything that happened there. I shouldn't be thinking about my next steps. I just killed my father. What I do tomorrow should be the least of my concerns, but I welcome the distraction even if it's riddled with worry.

I don't want to leave Grimm, but I don't know if either of us is ready for me to move in. He didn't even sleep in the bed with me last night. After washing me in his tub and changing me into one of his t-shirts and boxer shorts, he cuddled me, smoothing my hair down as I cried myself to sleep. I awoke in the middle of the night to find him gone, too tired from my sobbing to go search for him. And now that it's morning and he's still not here, I know that he never returned to my side.

I suppose he wanted to give me space to grieve. I probably need it, but being pressed up against him is much more comfortable. The thought of his hard body against mine, his dark eyes, the scruff poking under her skin—combine it all with the smell wafting around me, and it's already too much. Perhaps I just want a reprieve from the sorrow, a more pleasurable distraction, but I don't care about the motives. I need him. I need his hands on me to make me feel nothing but pleasure.

As if my desire summoned him, the bedroom door creaks open, and Grimm pokes his head in. I sit up as he enters, a tray full of food in his hands. "I brought you breakfast," he says, his voice slow and cautious.

I'm delighted to find him void of his usual, put-together appearance. He wears plaid navy sleep shorts and a loose gray t-shirt. He takes a seat on the bed, passes me the tray of food, and flips out the little legs, so I have a makeshift table. "I'm not hungry," I say, brushing a strand of hair behind my ear.

"You need to eat." He's right, of course, but my stomach doesn't shake with hunger when looking down at his beautifully-prepared meal. It does incite another sort of hunger in me. Looking at him—I'm ravenous. I don't want to be rude after he prepared all of this for me, although I've been nothing but rude since the day I met the man; it's obviously different now. I grab a crispy piece of bacon and bring it up to my lips, taking a small bite.

"How are you feeling?"

I shrug, not knowing how to respond. Instead, I push the food aside and reach for him, running my hands over his hard chest. I bring my lips to his neck, kissing him softly.

"Ember," he says through a pained moan. "I don't know if this is such a good idea."

"It's a good idea to me." I kiss his lips.

He's hesitant at first, but it's obvious he can't deny me for long. His mouth opens, and his tongue explores me. He pulls back just a millimeter. "Are you sure?"

"I've never been more sure."

His arms wrap around me, and he pulls me onto his lap. I grind against his length, already so hard for me. His hands reach for my breasts over my shirt, and I frantically grab the bottom of the large fabric, pulling away from his lips to pull the material over my head. He snaps me against him once I'm free, but I push back. It's not good enough. I need to feel him completely. I'm desperate to remove his clothes, needing his warmth. He doesn't deny me any of my silent requests, quickly discarding his t-shirt and sleep shorts before pulling off his boxers I'm wearing.

I'm bare on top of him, letting my slick cunt glide against his cock, his knot at the base. I shouldn't be thinking about anything besides his release inside of me, but I can't help but replay Red's remarks about mates. My body and soul are on fire. It would only make sense that we're made for each other.

Of course, I want him inside of me, stretching my inner walls until I'm finally rid of the emptiness, but my mouth waters for more. I push him back against the bed. His forehead scrunches as he watches me crawl down him. "Ember, you don't need to do that."

"I want to taste you, Grimm."

He surrenders, falling back against the bed with a heavy breath. I've never taken a man in my mouth before—I never even thought it would appeal to me, but holding his pleasure on my lips feels so powerful, something I'm desperate to gain when nothing but weakness coats my bones. I take just the tip of him, lathering him with my tongue.

"Fuck, Ember!" he cries, holding my shoulders. Surely I can't be that good at this. I've barely even started, but the encouragement makes me eager to be even better, to blow his mind as well as his cock.

I take more of him, rolling my lips down his shaft, using all the tongue I can while keeping my lips as tight as possible.

"Why are you so good at this?" he asks, pained and delirious.

Is he just trying to make me feel good? I don't care because it's working. My legs slip against each other as I work him in and out of my mouth. I grab his balls since I've always been curious about the weight of him, massaging them and shifting to his knot.

"Fuck no," he jerks upright, pushing me back so I'm lying on my back.

"What?" I say, panicked, sure I did something wrong.

He pushes my legs apart, pinning me down and running his finger along my seam. "I'm about to come down your throat."

My nerves release, all of me opens as he presses into me, his fingers dancing in my tender valley. "So? Maybe I want that?"

"I won't be fully satisfied until you're crying out in pleasure. If you want to fuck to drive the pain away,

I'll fuck you, happily, but I won't do so unless you're delirious with ecstasy."

How can I refuse him? My body relaxes as I sink into the thick comforter beneath me. He peppers kisses down my neck until he reaches my breasts, sucking, biting, and teasing as he runs rings around the sensitive bud at the top of my sex. It's only a matter of minutes before my nerves melt into an urgent release. I'm screaming as my body tightens, wanting to be filled but welcoming the soul-sucking pleasure passing through me.

"Fuck me, please!" I gag on the words, my release not depleted, but I need the fullness, need the connection. He doesn't waver, moving his hand and thrusting into me, quick and urgent.

I scratch his back, and he cries out into the crook of my neck as he drives himself home. It's rough—not as much as last time—but the last bit of myself I was holding back releases. His knot stretches my opening as he spills into me, applying the perfect amount of pleasure mixed with pain. Just as I suspected, I feel whole. I wonder if it will feel the same once he deflates and slips out of me.

He pecks tender kisses over the side of my face, pushing my hair aside. This isn't like the other two times before, three if you count when he fucked me with his hand in his living room. This is special. No secrets are pushing us apart; it's just him and me connected.

All at once, I know the feeling, the words bubbling up from deep within me before I can stop them. "I love you," I say around an exhale.

Grimm stiffens atop me. I didn't register my words, but now that they're out, I know they're true. I should be happy about my discovery, but Grimm doesn't reply. He straightens his arms, holding himself over me with a look of concern. I didn't say the words to hear them back, but it's obvious he doesn't plan to reciprocate my feelings.

It shouldn't sting. It's too soon even to utter the phrase, let alone actually feel them—this is my first relationship, and I barely know him, but I can't deny the pain. He looks at me as if he pities me.

Tears well in my eyes. I'm surprised I even have any left. "Ember, please don't cry." He cradles my face, but I turn out of his grasp. It's obvious to me now that he doesn't feel the same way. He would have told me if he did.

He pops free, pulling out of me, as if my confession caused his knot to deflate, but he doesn't stop touching me, running his fingers through my hair in a way of comfort. "You're not thinking straight. It's too soon..." I push him off of me, stopping his words. I don't want to hear anymore. Of course, he's right, but it doesn't stop the fact that my feelings are real—bright and blinding and they must burn without tinder, threatening to consume all of me. I need space, to get away and clear my head. He doesn't mean to hurt me. He's trying to offer me comfort, but it's not working, and he's breaking me instead.

I roll off the bed, collecting the clothes he lent me off the floor and pulling them on.

"Ember, please don't go. Let's talk about this. There's still so much you don't know."

I straighten, holding my hand to him but unable to look him in the eye. "I don't want to hear it right now. I just need to clear my head."

"Of course, whatever you need," he says, kneeling on the edge of the bed, but his muscles are straining as if he wants to pull me back.

"Is the guest house cleaned up?"

He pauses, registering what I'm asking. "Yes, but Ember…"

"Okay, I'm going back there for the day. Just give me time to think."

"I don't know if that's a good idea."

"I need my own space."

He's silent for a moment. "Of course, whatever you need."

I storm out of the room, exiting the house barefoot and heading toward my cottage—the place I killed my father. I should be squirming out of my skin at the thought of what I've done and what this means, but all I care about is Grimm—the man I love who doesn't love me back.

22

GRIMM

I gave her some time to calm down. I'm unsure if it's the right decision or not, but I can't make this about me when she's going through so much. The hours weighed heavily on my nerves. She left without me clarifying. I don't blame her. She's dealing with her new self, the loss of her father, and the unknown implications our bond has on her emotions. She's still not fully aware of the magnitude between us. I need to tell her, but I worry it's not the time. Of course, I can't have her hurting more, and it seems that keeping the truth from her does just that.

The guest cottage door is cracked open, and I slip inside. I should make myself known, but when I see her form through the slit between the bedroom door and its hinge, a lump covered in the white comforter, I creep inside instead.

The cleanup crew did a good job. I can't even tell what happened here just the day before. It's a relief. It hurts to imagine Ember's reaction if she walked into any evidence of the carnage.

I push my way into the bedroom. I crawl into the bed, wrapping her in my arms. Every cell aches to have her near. She's the second piece of my heart—my mate. I must be by her, even if only rejection comes next.

To my delight, she burrows into me, her body warm and relaxed. I brush her hair behind her ear, kissing the side of her face. She turns around to face me, her eyes puffy and red-rimmed. "I'm sorry. I shouldn't have run out like that. It was immature."

I kiss her forehead, holding her closer. "Don't apologize. You're entitled to however your feelings come and go, especially now."

She presses her face into my chest, inhaling me. I smile, taking my own sniff of her strawberry custard-scented hair. I hope we can lie like this for the last few hours of the day, letting the horizon swallow the sun and carry us into a blissful sleep. Of course I'd want more than that. I must arch my lower half back slightly to not poke her. But that can come later. Just holding her is more than enough.

"What happens now?" she asks.

"With what?"

"My father's death? What does this mean for us? I'm assuming it won't be easy to sweep under the rug."

"The DOS will handle it. I just talked to them. They're claiming it as suicide after the new video surfaced."

"You think that will work?"

"Yes." Of course, there are intricacies to this plan, but I don't want to worry her with the details. She deserves some relief.

She nods, accepting my answer, but from the way her eyes track in their sockets, I can tell there is more she wants to say. Finally, she parts her lips. "You don't have to love me yet."

It breaks my heart. I cup her chin, bringing her attention to me. "It's not that. It's more than that."

She scrunches her face.

Why is it so hard to just come out with it? "It's more than love. You're my mate. I know you might not know what that means, but it's a predestined pairing. We're made for each other. I didn't realize it at first. I think it's because you're only part, so the sensation wasn't as obvious to me. But when we had sex for the first time, and I knotted you, that's when I knew. I should have told you sooner, but I was scared. I'd rather live a life without you than force you into a life you don't want."

She strokes my face. "I know."

"You know?"

"Red explained what mates were the other day." Her cheeks bloom. "Knotting and such. I didn't think it could be true, but a piece of me knew right away. Hearing you say the words put everything in place."

"And how do you feel about that? About being mated to an old man like me?"

"How do you feel about being mated to someone as immature as me?"

"You're not immature."

She shoots me a look. "I don't even know how to swim."

I smile. "I'll gladly teach you, along with a few other things." I brush my lips over hers.

"Should I wear a schoolgirl outfit whenever we're in session?" I cup her ass, pulling her against me. "I'd prefer you wear nothing." She kisses me, framed with a smile.

God, do I want to push myself inside of her, relieve the ache of my knot, but there are still things left unsaid. I pull back. "I love you."

She rolls her eyes. "You don't have to say it."

"No, but it's true, except it's so much more than that. You're a part of me, Ember, the fibers of my being. It's too much to explain exactly how I feel."

"Then show me, show me how much you love me."

I hook under her leg, wrapping it around me. "I plan to every day, for the rest of our lives."

"You promise?" she asks, breath against my lips.

"I promise."

We embrace—not for the first time—but this is different from all the rest. We're mated, claimed, and there's nothing uncertain about our feelings for each other. The wolf lies with the fox who snuck into his heart and burrowed herself a home.

23

EMBER

One Year Later

I push myself forward, the cool water grazing my skin, relieving the heat from the midday sun above me. When it's deep enough, I flip to my back, floating on the surface of the lake as the water laps around me. I swim in the lake every day now. It's wild to me that I went twenty years of my life without experiencing the bliss that is floating on the surface of cool, still waters. It only took Grimm a few weeks to teach me. He said I learn fast, but I think he's just a good teacher. He made it fun. Told me if I could reach him in the middle, he'd let me suck his cock. Seemed like a win-win for him, but he knows all too well how eager I am to have my lips around his shaft.

"Ember!" his voice pierces through the barrier of the water, and I sit up to look at him, waving at me from the edge of the lawn. "Time to eat!" he calls. Partygoers line up behind him at the grill, white plates and empty hot dog buns in hand.

My stomach rumbles as I swim back to shore, waving to a few pack members sprinkled across the green, tanning with beers in hand. Children dance along the tide, playing tag or tackling each other into the water. Some shift into their Were-form every few moments, not used to their powers yet. All the Were-children are of the wolf variant, although I surmise Brick and Carmen's child might take on some pig features. I can't help wondering what Grimm and my children will look like. Probably more wolf, since my fox self is so minuscule. Although, Grimm loves to remind me how powerful I am, and that it's just the beginning of my untapped powers surfacing.

I run the rest of the distance to my mate. Grimm stretches out an arm to me as I approach, and I curl myself into him. His white linen shirt is fully unbuttoned to reveal his muscular chest. His swim shorts are dry now from his earlier dip in the lake, but he doesn't seem to mind my wet body pressed against him. He kisses the top of my forehead, listening to Cameron as he rambles on about his daughter, Christine's, already impressive pattern recognition abilities.

"Here, I got you a plate," Grimm interrupts, handing me a hot dog already dressed in ketchup and mustard.

"Thank you," I smile, reaching to pull myself up to his lips.

He kisses me, biting my lip before releasing me. I shove the hot dog in my mouth, taking a bite without letting my stare leave his. It's corny—him getting turned on as I eat a hot dog in my tiny pink bikini, me completely playing into it, eating slowly and unlike how a normal human would eat, but I swear I'm in heat or something because I can't stop thinking about sex with him. I guess it's been that way for the past year, though. I can't get enough of my mate.

"Slow down over there, or you'll end up like me," Red says as she waddles toward us, one hand on her rounded belly and the other holding the tiny hand of Christine. I don't say the truth, that I want to end up like her. I'm only twenty-one, but I'm desperate to carry a litter of Grimm's children. Maybe it's because everyone around me is pregnant or having babies, but it's more likely biological—a Were's desire to procreate. Hopefully, this hot dog action will lead to me getting impregnated later today. I have half the mind to scarf the rest down and pull Grimm into the woods, but we have company, and Brick, Cameron, and their little one join our group huddle.

Cameron leans over to Red, pretending to whisper but in a way that everyone hears. "Ya know, I'm the reason those two were together. I could sense a connection between them the first time they met."

Grimm rolls his eyes with a laugh and slaps Cameron's shoulder. "Yes, thank you for butting it."

I smile before noticing Carmen walking closer to the group. "Did he nap?" I ask once she's close enough—her brown-haired, wide-eyed baby slung across her hip.

"No," she grumbles. "He's very finicky about where he naps."

I thought the guest house would be a perfect place for Carter to get some peace and quiet, but the baby boy looks happy and active.

Brick reaches for the baby. "Here, give him to me. Eat a hot dog. Take a dip in the lake, come out of the water all slow-like, and I'll stay here and watch."

Carmen clucks with an eye roll and a smile before handing Carter to Brick. "Fine, but behave yourself while I cool off real quick." She kisses him on the lips and saunters to the lake, rocking her hips in her brown bikini. Maybe we're all in heat right now.

Brick watches her go, baby in one hand, red solo cup in the other.

Cameron slaps his chest. "Ew, please not in front of me. That's my sister, remember?"

Brick doesn't tear his eyes away. "Gettt over it."

Grimm chuckles, pulling me closer. "Any news, Brick?" he asks. A year ago, this wouldn't have been an appropriate topic of conversation at a party. Everything was tense, dangerous, and unknown. Now, with the Hunters no more than a small and publicly-despised hate group, news from the DOS isn't as high-stakes. A year ago, after the death of my father, the DOS orchestrated a press release detailing my father's "suicide." Senator Green wasn't the only high-profile member of the Hunters hiding in the government, but after the video I posted, coupled with Carmen's resurgent exposé, the public had a different view on the Hunters and werewolves. People were rioting on our behalf, starting fundraisers to support the Weres affected by the brutality of Hunters. Sure, there were still people who sided with the Hunters and feared us for our otherness, but the young, justice-seeking people of America's voices were heard, and policies were quickly put in place to protect us.

It's still not perfect. My people are still discriminated against, violence is still prevalent, and the fear among my pack still weighs heavily. But I like to imagine a world where humans and Weres can live together in harmony, and the old prejudiced farts die out for good. I think the hopeful future is making everyone have baby fever right about now. Carmen told me the other day that she wants to try again in about six months.

Brick shrugs. "Nothing to be concerned about. They're flying me out to DC for a press conference next weekend." He groans. "I told them this is the last trip I'm taking for a while. I'm thankful I still have my job with them, but they can't keep toting me around to prove that people's tax dollars are being well-managed."

"Oh, Ember," Red says. "I loved that video you posted yesterday to the feed."

I hit Grimm with my hip. "Did you hear that? She loved it." As the new—and first— social media manager for the Dayton Werewolf Council, I take my job very seriously. This includes staying up to date on the latest trends and dance moves, making short videos of the pack members to show the public that we're just like everyone else. Grimm always groans whenever I try to pull him into a video with me, but it doesn't take much convincing to get him to agree to my antics.

"I told you it was brilliant." He kisses the top of my forehead.

"Yeah, but I knew you thought it was stupid."

"It doesn't matter what I think. I don't know what people are into nowadays."

"How many views is it at?" Cameron asks.

"Last I checked, we had two million," I answer.

Cameron chuckles. "Damn, who knew that all we needed was for Grimm to do a little dance to make us go viral?"

Grimm pulls me tighter to his side. "No, all we need is Ember. She's the brains behind it. Besides, I think everyone was looking at her dancing next to me with her cute little ears and tail."

"Oh, stop." I slap his chest, my cheeks blooming. He's not lying, though. I keep checking the comments. I've acquired quite a following due to my fox features. Sometimes it weirds me out that people love seeing my Were-form, but a larger part of me finds the positive attention incredibly healing. I don't need the world to love me, though. I have my mate who loves me no matter what form I take.

Love for my man overtakes me. I've got to get out of the eyes of others. "Oh, Grimm. I forgot to tell you, I think I saw some sort of animal digging up the flower beds around the cottage."

Our bond is thick. "Oh, really? Yikes, I just planted those. You'd better show me where you saw it." He doesn't even question why I'd bring up such a silly topic in the company of our friends.

I smile, leading him away from the group. "Ya, know you could just say you guys are leaving to fuck instead of coming up with some weak narrative," Cameron yells from behind us.

"Fuck off!" Grimm doesn't even turn to throw his insult, quickening his steps and dragging me along. I want to remind him that I'm supposed to be the one showing him something, not the other way around, but I guess the jig is up anyway. I run along with him, giggling as we make it into the cover of the treeline.

We're barely into the woods when Grimm shoves me against a tall tree, one hand groping my bikini top and the other wrapped around my waist as he brings his hot mouth to mine. He breaks away, bringing his lips to my ears as he frees my breast from my top. "God, you smell so good, Ember. You're so juicy for me, I could barely last another second."

I laugh. "Juicy? What am I, a steak?"

"Yes, a steak I can't wait to sink my teeth in."

I try to grind against him, needing him to relieve the heat inside of me, but he pushes me back against the tree, kissing down the expanse of my body until he's kneeling on the floor. He flings my legs over his shoulders, and I yelp as I'm pushed higher. I brace myself, claws digging into the bark as his tongue laps across my inner thighs. He pulls my bikini bottoms to the side, his breath on my sopping core. "God, Grimm. Please!" I beg, not even concerned about how loud I'm being and how we're not nearly far enough into the woods.

"I need to taste my mate." He groans before licking through me. "God, you taste so good. I could spend the rest of my days between your legs, licking up the new moisture I summon from you."

I reach for his salt-and-pepper hair, urging him to continue his laps. Something changes, and I don't even need to look down to know that he shifted his face into his Were-form. The tongue that laps through me is incredibly long and ridged. He inserts a finger inside of me—a human finger, as the claws would likely do some damage. The wolf eats my pussy greedily and without playing games. I cry out, attempting to muffle my screams now with the back of my hand. I barely even notice that my ears and tail have popped free until Grimm grabs my ass and strokes the fur from my tail, just as he turns his attention to my clit. My body melts beneath him, and I buck as my release washes over me.

He continues stroking me until I've slackened and not a second more. He returns my feet to the ground and flips me over so my ass is pressed against him. He shimmies out of his swim shorts with quick accuracy, his hardened cock rubbing against my ass like he can't last another second without the friction. Confirming my thoughts, his gruff voice tickles at the shell of my ear. "I can't wait anymore. I need to fill you."

"Take me. Breed me. Ruin me."

He pulls my bikini bottom down my damp legs before thrusting inside of me. I cry out from the abrupt force, but the pain quickly turns to pleasure as fast as it came. He's wild, driving into me, the sound of his skin slapping against mine, the wetness from my cunt as my walls greedily pull him deeper—it washes my mind of reason, turns me into a vessel of pleasure, breathing for nothing more than to be fucked by my mate.

His thrusts become even more frantic, and I must use all my force to prevent my face from skimming against the rough bark of the tree. He reaches a deep part in me, so deep I don't think he's ever tapped into before. Stars cloud my vision, and the world goes black around me. All I can register is the warmth of his seed filling me up even more, going deeper than what should be possible for my body to contain. I'm lost as Grimm's knot expands within me, tying me to him and refusing to let even a morsel of him drip out.

He brings my awareness back through the peppering of kisses across my back. "Ember, I love you. I love you," he murmurs over and over again, gently pulling me to the blanket of leaves beneath us. I come to myself while lying next to him, his arms pulling me close, and his lips kissing down the side of my face. "Are you okay?" he asks. "Was that too rough?" He always asks me the same question when he fucks the consciousness out of me, and I always have the same answer. "It was fucking fantastic."

"I think I might have really done it this time," he says around a sigh. "Put a baby in you."

I laugh. "I hope so."

"Are you sure?" His voice takes a serious tone.

I try to turn to him. Only my neck moves. "I told you I'm ready. Are you?"

"Of course." He tucks a strand of damp hair behind my ear. "Anything you offer me, I'll gobble up greedily. I just still have a hard time believing you'd want to give me such a precious gift."

I roll my eyes. "Please don't start with the *I'm so old* act. You know you're fucking hot."

"I don't know that I'm fucking hot."

"Good."

"Good?"

"Yeah, if you knew that it would ruin everything."

He laughs and continues his assault of kisses. "God, I love you, my mate."

"I love you too."

We lie in the orange leaves for as long as we can, until our skin prickles from the shaded wind and our packmates' calls grow louder. We right our bathing suits before exiting the privacy of the forest, smiling, hand in hand as we rejoin our pack, our family, and our home.

THANKS FOR READING!

Thank you for reading! If you liked *Bound to the Wolf: A Grimm Love Story*, make sure to leave a review.

Scream for Me: A Dark Monster Love Story

The harbinger of fear, the predator of the night...

I feast on human terror, drinking in their screams like the sweetest nectar. But when I stumble through the portal into her room and hear her cries of pleasure, a far darker, primal hunger takes hold.

She belongs to me now. I need to hear her scream like that again, and I will, even if I have to break her apart.

The woman stolen from her world and thrust into a realm of nightmares...

I felt it—eyes watching me from the darkness, golden and unblinking from the shadows of my closet. The thought sent a shiver through me, twisting into something illicit as I let my fingers wander. But when he pounced, dragging me into his cold, merciless world, the thrill turned to terror.

Now, he demands my pleasure, my screams, but I refuse to surrender without a fight.

Step Brother Bear: A Bear Shifter Lover Story
Her step-brother is an animal, and she is his prey.

Isabella has always hated her unruly step-brother, Derek. Luckily for her, he spent most of their lonely upbringings at a boarding school for troubled kids. Now that she's an adult and back in her childhood home, she hates the tattooed, moody man even more. Mostly because he's right next door, set on making her life miserable and behaving like a literal animal. Things get even worse when her mom and step-dad leave town and task her to care for the beast and his newly acquired gunshot wounds. Their close quarters reveal heated secrets with monstrous consequences. There's more to Derek than meets the eye, leaving Isabella to excavate terrifying and confusing feelings.

Can she see past the claws, or will she decide the two are just entirely different species?

Stay up to date on all things G.M. Fairy!